Street Cop II

Reloaded

DAVID SPELL

RESOURCE *Publications* · Eugene, Oregon

STREET COP II
Reloaded

Copyright © 2011 David Spell. All rights reserved. Except for brief quotations in critical publications or reviews, no part of this book may be reproduced in any manner without prior written permission from the publisher. Write: Permissions, Wipf and Stock Publishers, 199 W. 8th Ave., Suite 3, Eugene, OR 97401.

Resource Publications
An Imprint of Wipf and Stock Publishers
199 W. 8th Ave., Suite 3
Eugene, OR 97401
www.wipfandstock.com

ISBN 13: 978-1-61097-652-7
Manufactured in the U.S.A.

*To My Father, Charles T. Spell, Jr.
He delivered the mail for over forty-seven years.
He set an incredible example for me for both
Hard work and public service. He and my mother, Patricia, have been
Married for fifty years. Their marriage is a lasting
Example of love and faithfulness.*

Contents

Preface ix

1. Signal 63 • 1
2. Chasing Ghosts • 9
3. Coked Up Body Builder • 13
4. Inclimate Weather and Idiots • 17
5. Drunk Drivers • 22
6. Training, Training, Training • 31
7. Accident on the Interstate • 38
8. I See Dead People • 42
9. A Midnight Swim • 51
10. Violent Crack Head • 56
11. Tough Guy • 62
12. Just Another Afternoon in the Trailer Park • 65
13. When You Gotta Go . . . • 68
14. Raising Children or Creating Monsters? • 71
15. Another Vicious Dog • 78
16. Alligator on the Loose • 81
17. The Cop and the Kitty • 85
18. Weird Stuff • 91

19 Prostitutes, Midgets, and Drugs: Busting a Mexican Bordello • 95

20 Most Embarrassing Moments • 100

21 Drunk on a Riding Mower • 108

22 Nino and the Stolen Car • 112

23 Firepower • 120

    Epilogue • 129

Preface

When *Street Cop* came out in 2010, the question that I kept hearing was, "When are you going to write another police book?" I really had not planned on doing a second *Street Cop* book but that repeated question forced me to dig back into my nearly thirty years as a police officer and deal with some more repressed memories. I think that is the nature of any biographical writing. Some of the stories recounted here are still painful. The chapter, "Accident on the Interstate," talks about a serious car wreck I was in. My police car was totaled. I was almost totaled myself. My back never fully recovered from that impact. The chapter, "I See Dead People," talks about a couple of homicides scenes that I was at. I don't think anyone can see some of the things that I discuss and not be scarred.

There are plenty of funny moments here as well. If you don't laugh or at least smile when you get to the chapter, "Prostitutes, Midgets, and Drugs: Busting a Mexican Bordello," something is wrong with you. I have also included several chapters here that I was hesitant to include in the first *Street Cop*. I do not want to offend anybody but, at the same time, these are all real events that are going on all around us, even in our nice suburban neighborhoods. The chapter, "Weird Stuff" is a great example of that. You might feel the conflicting emotions of amusement and disgust at the same time. Welcome to my world.

As with the previous book, all of these stories are true. I have supplemented my memory with police reports, news clippings, Google, and informal chats with some of the other officers who appear in these chapters. As before, I have only included officer's first names. I have also changed suspect's names and cleaned up the dialogue a bit. Some of these stories will amuse you, others will disturb you. My goal, however, is still the same. I want you to have a greater appreciation for the men and women in blue that place their lives on the line every day to protect us all from the predators that roam among us.

Special thanks to Scott Calman Studio for the back cover photo. Scott is a brilliant photographer and good friend. He even made me look presentable!

David Spell
Buford, Georgia
July, 2011

1

Signal 63

It was late August of 1989. I was working the midnight shift in the Snellville area. It was a slow night so there were four of us hanging out together in an empty parking lot and drinking coffee. Lieutenant Wally, Officer Diane, Officer Bob and myself were responsible for the area that today has at least ten officers assigned to it. The police radio was quiet and we were enjoying a few minutes of peace. We had been standing outside, leaning against our patrol cars and chatting for about twenty minutes.

At about one in the morning, the silence was broken as the dispatcher hit the alert tone to get our attention and then keyed up and said, "All units, Signal 63. Officers are fighting with numerous subjects and request immediate backup. All units, Signal 63." She provided the address to a location in the next district over in Norcross. Most police departments use number signals when talking on the radio. The reason for this is to allow the officer or dispatcher to say what they need to say in as few words as possible. Some signals are heard all the time and become commonplace. A Signal 63, however, is one of those signals that is rarely ever heard. I could probably count on one hand the number of times in my almost thirty years that I have heard an officer put out a Signal 63.

Most of the time, we send two officers on any call that sounds like it has the potential for violence. Other calls may require two officers just because it might be a confusing or complicated scene. A serious car wreck may require a second officer to direct traffic while the first officer works the accident. There are many other times when an officer will be by himself on a call or a traffic stop and then realize that they might need some help. When that happens, the first officer will simply call for a car in an adjoining zone to come and join him. He has requested backup but in a very low key manner.

There are other times, however, when an officer is on a call or on a traffic stop and everything suddenly falls apart. An example would be of an officer who suddenly finds himself in a physical struggle with a suspect while trying to arrest them. The officer needs immediate help, but two or three more officers will probably be able to get the situation under control. Our signal in that situation is a "Code 7." When an officer requests a Code 7, everyone in the immediate area will start towards them. Usually, after the first two or three officers have arrived and gotten the situation under control, all the other cars will be cancelled. A Code 7 is a priority call, but it would be rare to have officers from another precinct responding as a backup.

When an officer puts out a Signal 63, however, the situation is dire. It implies that if they don't get backup right away, there is a good chance that an officer is going to be seriously hurt or worse. It is the most serious radio signal in our vocabulary. Each of our five precincts have their own radio channel. When an officer calls out "Signal 63" over the air, the dispatcher will transmit it over each of the other four radio channels. The city police departments will also be contacted. In an extremely bad situation, all of the surrounding county jurisdictions will be notified of the Signal 63 so that their officers can respond as well. I had never been on a Signal 63 or any other call that had been that bad. If you have to start calling for surrounding agencies for help, things have gotten really serious.

This was in 1989. We were not dealing with many of the issues that police departments have to be aware of today. This was before the active shooters at Columbine High School. This was before the Islamic terror threat had taken the center stage of world affairs. At that time, I could not imagine an incident that would require the contacting of other Metro Atlanta police departments to come and help us. I was about to have my imagination expanded.

When we heard the Signal 63, we all dashed to get in our police cars. Lieutenant Wally said, "Spell, you and Bob start over there. Diane and I will hold the fort down over here." I could see the disappointment on Diane's face. She wanted to go help out also. But the Lieutenant was right. We could not leave an entire area of the county unprotected. We were not close to the call and I think we all thought that the Signal 63 would be cancelled before Bob and I ever got there.

Bob and I turned on our blue lights and sirens and started across the county. We flipped over to the radio channel of the district that we were responding to. When we changed radio channels, we immediately heard a voice screaming, "Radio, we need some help! We are having to fight multiple subjects." When the officer transmitted, I could hear yelling and screaming in the background. It sounded like the officer was in the middle of a riot.

Bob and I were driving as fast as we dared. Thankfully, there was not much traffic on the road at that late hour. I was in the lead and tried to navigate the quickest way to the call. Over the radio, I could hear the first backup units starting to arrive at the scene. Within just a few minutes, five backup units had arrived. *They will probably cancel us in a few more minutes*, I thought. Instead of cancelling us, though, another officer keyed up his radio and screamed over the yelling voices in the background, "Signal 63! Signal 63! This is still an active fight! We need more officers!"

Bob and I continued to drive hard, pushing our police cars to their limit. We continued to hear backup units getting to the call. After a few more minutes, the dispatcher tried to raise an officer over the radio to see if they were okay. "Negative, radio! We are all engaged. We still need more officers!" *What are Bob and I walking into? I wondered. How do you have a riot in the middle of a nice, middle class neighborhood?*

Finally, after fifteen minutes of intense driving we got there. By now, there were close to thirty police cars on the scene from several different jurisdictions and Bob and I had to park down the street. We grabbed our flashlights and nightsticks and started up the road. There was no question as to which house we were going to. We could hear the yelling and see several different fights taking place at the same time in the front yard. *Where do we start?* All of the officers that we saw who were fighting with suspects, looked okay. There were two or three officers per bad guy and it looked like they were trying to get their guys handcuffed.

There was an open door on the side of the house that led into the basement. We could hear yelling inside so Bob and I headed for the open door. The basement was partially finished. There were sofas, chairs and a couple of beds scattered around the large room. I saw a set of stairs on the other side of the basement that led up into the house.

Our first job was to find the primary officers and find out how we could help. We could hear yelling, as well as the sounds of something, or someone, being slammed around upstairs. Bob and I started across the room for the stairs. There was a wet bar against the wall to our left. A black guy had been hiding behind it. He stood up and saw us. He raised the middle finger of both hands toward us and said something unkind about our lineage. It was obvious that he was drunk, but his English was also heavily accented. We found out later that everyone at the party was from Liberia in West Africa.

Quickly, Bob and I turned to the left and went to deal with the drunk guy. We did not want him sneaking up behind us later. At this same time, I heard a struggle at the top of the basement stairs. It sounded like someone had just been slammed into a wall. There were several Liberian voices screaming in unison at the top of the stairs. Then I heard two sets of footsteps running down the stairs. A second later I saw another party goer get down to the basement and start running for the open door. The pursuing officer was only a few steps behind him. I stepped in front of the Liberian blocking his escape. He decided that rather than trying to go around me, he was going to go through me. Bad idea. As he charged me, I hit him in the face with my right forearm. It had the same effect as if he had been clothes-lined. His head snapped back and his feet went out from under him. The guy was knocked on his butt. He immediately tried to scramble to his feet. The pursuing officer and I tackled him, with all three of us landing on a nearby bed. Our combined weight caused the slats on the bed to break. The box springs and the mattress collapsed onto the floor. The bad guy was quickly handcuffed and the first officer said that he could get him out to his police car without any assistance.

I turned my attention back to Bob just in time to see him bounce the drunk perp that he was dealing with off of the bar and then handcuff him. I asked him if he needed any help getting his prisoner out to the car. At that moment, we heard what sounded like another person slammed to the floor over our heads. There was still a lot of yelling from upstairs.

Bob said, "I should be okay. Why don't you go see if you can help out up there?"

When I got to the top of the stairs into the main level of the house, I saw an officer chasing another drunk Liberian through the house and up the stairs. By now, most of the people were realizing that the police meant business and it probably was not a good idea to get in our way.

About ten Liberians were sitting on couches, chairs, and the floor in the living room, making no effort to help their fleeing friend out. I ran up the stairs and found Officer Mike inside of a bedroom. The man that he had been chasing had jumped onto a bed and was being held protectively by a drunk Liberian woman. She said, "No, you cannot take him," and then wrapped her arms tightly around him.

Officer Mike paused a moment, staring at the crazy situation. He was out of breath and I found out later that he was one of the first officers on-scene. I pointed at the guy on the bed and asked, "Is he under arrest?"

"Oh yeah. This is his house. He is the one who threw this party. He started all of this," Mike answered.

I spoke to the woman on the bed, "Lady, you can let him go or you can go to jail, too."

She said, "He hasn't done anything wrong. You can't take him."

You had your chance, I thought.

"I'll grab her," I told Mike. "I'll peel her off and deal with her and you grab the guy and get him handcuffed."

Another officer joined us in the bedroom and heard the plan. I reached behind the woman and grabbed a handful of hair and used it to turn her head. At the same time, I grabbed the little finger on her left hand and bent it back.

She screamed at me, "No!"

She then let go of the love of her life and came after me. She tried to hit me with her free arm and even tried to bite me. I kicked her feet out from under her and dropped her on her face on the bedroom floor. I dropped my knees into her back and heard her scream, "Stop! You are hurting me!"

"Put your hands behind your back," I ordered.

"Someone, please help me!" the Liberian woman yelled.

She refused to put her hands behind her. This time, I grabbed the little finger on her right hand and pulled it back for effect. She screamed in pain. "Give me your other hand," I ordered, and increased the pressure almost to the breaking point.

The drunk woman finally put her left hand behind her and I was able to get her handcuffed. At the same time that I was dealing with her, Mike and the other officer dragged the drunk Liberian man off the bed and onto the floor. He had resisted briefly but a few well-placed strikes caused him to cease struggling and allow himself to be handcuffed. We escorted both subjects downstairs and then outside. When we got outside, we were awash in a sea of blue lights. I found out later that there were over sixty police cars there from about ten different jurisdictions. Several Deputies from our Sherriff's Department had also come to help. One was driving a transport van. It was already almost full. The male and female that we put in the van made a total of thirteen Liberians that were arrested.

The thirteen prisoners were charged with a variety of offenses including Disorderly Conduct, Resisting Arrest, and Simple Battery. The owner of the house was also charged with Maintaining a Disorderly House, since he was the one who had thrown the party. Most of the party goers had left by now. Many cars were left behind because so many of them were blocked in by police cars. We figured people must have caught rides with friends who could get to their cars.

Now that the scene was stabilized, we got the whole story from Officer Bill and Officer Mike. They had gone to the location about an hour earlier in response to a complaint of a loud party. The first time they were out there, they had spoken to the homeowner and had given him a warning about the noise. The Liberian man had assured them that he would turn the music down and try and get the crowd under control.

When the officers got another call to the same address about a loud party, they knew that they were going to have to do something. They both noticed, however, that the crowd was bigger this time. There had to be at least two hundred people crowded into the guy's house and spilling over into the yard. When they got there the second time, they asked some of the people who were standing in the front yard drinking beer, where the owner of the house was. The drunk Africans pointed them to the basement.

The basement door was standing open and there was a big group inside drinking and listening to some very loud West African reggae music. When the two officers walked into the basement, it took them a couple of minutes to locate the homeowner. They finally spotted him through the crowd on the other side of the basement. As they started towards him, Mike and Bill heard the basement door slam shut behind them. At the same time, someone turned the lights off, plunging the basement into darkness.

This was not a good place for the two officers to be. Most of the crowd panicked and tried to get out. A few people in the crowd used the darkness to take some cheap shots at the officers. Fortunately, no blows connected solidly, but they both took a few punches to the back and head. In return, the officers, standing back-to-back in the dark, started swinging their nightsticks and metal flashlights wildly around them. They were rewarded with several solid connections and a few squeals of pain. This was the point when Officer Bill was able to call out the Signal 63.

During this chaos, the owner of the house slipped upstairs. Someone finally opened the outside basement door again letting some light in. Mike and Bill were able to escape out into the yard. They went around to the front of the house. By now, the drunks at the party understood that Mike and Bill were looking for the homeowner. A few of the drunks stood blocking the front door. They told Mike and Bill that they could not come in. The officers had charges on the homeowner so they were not going to let a few drunk Africans (or a couple of hundred!) stop them. "Get out of the way or you're going to jail," Bill told them.

"You can't come in," one of the Liberians said.

At that moment, the first two backup police cars came roaring down the street with their blue lights and sirens on. They skidded to a stop and the officers jumped out ready for action. They saw Mike and Bill in front of the house. When the newcomers joined them, Mike and Bill started grabbing drunk Africans and the fight was on. When the rest of the crowd in the house saw that the police were laying hands on their friends, they started pouring out of the house. At first, officers were unable to get anyone handcuffed because they were just fighting to not get overwhelmed. As more and more officers arrived, however, they were able to grab and secure some of the more combative drunks. For the time being, they were just handcuffing them and putting them in the back of police cars. When the Sherriff's Department van got there later, the prisoners would be transferred to it.

Mike and Bill were not going to leave without the owner of the house. He was the one responsible for this crazy party and he needed to go to jail. Every time they tried to get in the house, though, they were being confronted by another drunk. Eventually, we had enough officers there to turn the tide. That was when the rest of the crowd realized that the smartest thing that they could do was to stay out of our way.

We could have easily arrested many more than the thirteen that we did. As it was we were very fortunate that none of the officers were injured. There were a few minor scratches and bruises, along with some ripped uniform shirts, but the police really held their own in this encounter. There were probably also a number of party goers that were able to get away bruised and bloodied from their encounter with Gwinnett's finest. They might have escaped arrest but their injuries would give them something to remember us by.

2

Chasing Ghosts

I HAD JUST GOTTEN a fresh cup of coffee. There was not much going on as I was starting another tour on the third shift. As I was pulling out of the convenience store parking lot south of Snellville, I noticed that the car in front of me, a black 1981 Datsun 280Z, did not have any tail lights. *He probably just has a blown fuse*, I thought. I would make a traffic stop and let them know that their tail lights were out. If his driver's license and insurance checked out, I would not even write him a citation.

I called the dispatcher and gave her my location and the vehicle's description. As I got closer, I noticed that the car did not have any license plates. There might be more to this than I had originally thought. I activated my blue lights and flicked my bright headlights on. The Datsun did not stop but just kept going down Highway 124 without changing speeds. Sometimes, when the blue lights came on, violators will freeze up, not knowing what to do or where to go. There were plenty of places to pull over on this stretch of road. We drove by a shopping center, a strip mall, and another convenience store but the Datsun still did not stop. I was close enough now that I could see into the interior of the vehicle with all of my lights activated. It looked like there were two young, white guys in the car.

The Datsun had not sped up so I did not think he was trying to get away from me. *Maybe he's drunk*, I thought. I reached over and turned on the siren. If the driver was drunk and just had not seen the flashing blue strobe lights behind him, it usually only took a second or two of the siren to get their attention. In this case, however, when the siren came on, it was like someone had waved a green flag in front of the driver of the Datsun. He floored it and began accelerating away from me.

I quickly notified the dispatcher that the vehicle had not stopped and that I was in pursuit. This was back in 1990 before our Pursuit Policy became very restrictive. The Datsun made a quick right turn onto Annistown Road. For the next couple of miles, this was a fairly straight section of road. The problem was that there was no way that my Ford Crown Victoria police car was going to be able to stay with the Datsun sports car. As I made the turn onto Annistown Road, I could see that he was already pulling away from me. There was no other traffic on the road and I had the accelerator pushed all the way to the floor.

Several other officers had heard my radio transmission and had said they were coming towards me from the other end of Annistown Road. I was just trying to keep the Datsun in sight. Since the fleeing car did not have any tail lights, this was not an easy task. There were side streets leading to neighborhoods all along this road. My biggest concern was that the fleeing Datsun would turn down one of these side streets and that I would lose him.

We were coming up on a sharp curve. Just after this curve, there was a bridge that crossed the Yellow River. My back up officers were still a minute or two away, but should meet us if the Datsun just kept going straight. The best thing that the responding officers could do would be to stop and wait for us. The Datsun was about five hundred yards ahead of me as it entered the sharp curve. There was a long straight away just past this curve that lead to the bridge across the river. As I came out of the curve, I was surprised to see empty road ahead of me. *Where did he go?* I wondered. It was like the car had just disappeared. Then, I saw blue lights coming from the other direction.

"Where did he go?" Officer Bart asked me over the radio.

"Didn't he pass you?" I asked him.

Bart and two other officers had been too close to have missed the Datsun if he had kept going straight. There were a couple of side streets near there and we all began checking them. I did not really believe the Datsun had turned off onto a side street. He had been going too fast. But where had he gone? We checked all the side streets and even drove down all the driveways for the houses along that stretch of road. It was like my fleeing Datsun had just disappeared. After about half an hour, we called off the search.

When our shift was over, we met back at the precinct to turn our paperwork in. Officer Bart walked up to me and said, "Hey, I understand. That is a great way to make those long nights go by a little quicker. Just make up a chase. That wakes us all up. That was a great idea!"

Bart was smiling, and I don't mind being the butt of a joke but I knew the other guys were wondering if I really had made the chase up. It did kind of look like it. The car had just vanished. I related the whole story to them but I could tell that they were not convinced. I briefed the Day Watch Sergeant just in case they came across the black Datsun, but I wasn't sure that he even believed me. I felt bad about losing the fleeing car, but I felt even worse knowing that the guys that I worked with were wondering if I had fabricated the whole chase story. In police work, you have to be able to trust the people that you are working with. Our lives are in each other's hands on a daily and nightly basis. That bothered me as I drove home and got ready for bed. I tossed and turned and did not sleep well that day.

When I woke up, I felt like I really had not slept at all. I wasn't rested and was already wondering what would happen when I went into to work that night. What was it going to take to win the guys' trust back? I had worked with these guys for a long time and they knew that I wasn't one to make stuff up. Still, this just did not look right.

My wife greeted me with a piece of paper after I had gotten out of bed. "Someone from work called for you. He wanted you to call him when you woke up," she said.

I looked at the note. It was from Officer Tim. He was a Day Watch officer at my precinct. *I wonder what he wants?* I picked up the phone and dialed the number. "Hey, David, we found your 280Z," he told me.

I was immediately awake. "What happened?" I asked.

Tim related the bizarre story to me. Later that morning, a motorist had noticed fresh tire marks leaving the roadway near the bridge over the Yellow River. This motorist thought that maybe someone had slid off of the road and had stopped to investigate. The helpful citizen had found the Datsun 280Z at the bottom of a steep hill, partially submerged in the Yellow River. There was no one with the car. Tim said that the marks would have been hard to see at night. There was also no way that we could have seen the car where it was at unless we had gotten out of our police cars and walked down the hill next to the bridge. And frankly, that thought had never occurred to me.

The citizen had called the police. Officer Tim had come to the scene and had impounded the Datsun. A check of the Vehicle Identification

Number revealed that the car had been reported stolen the previous day. I felt vindicated. No, I did not have a perp to arrest, but at least we had recovered a stolen car and the guys at work would know that I was not making crap up.

When I got to work that night a little after ten o'clock, the story had taken another bizarre twist. A father had called the police when his son showed up at the house wet, muddy, busted up, and with a broken leg. The family lived near the Yellow River and the son's story was that he had been in a car wreck near their home. The son, Brandon, had said he was with a friend who had driven off of the road, down a hill, and into the river. The friend had gotten scared and fled, leaving Brandon to fend for himself. Brandon knew his leg was hurt bad but said he had floated down the river until he was close to home. He then dragged himself out of the water and managed to limp home.

Brandon's perceptive father knew that something was amiss with his son's story and called the police. An Evening Watch officer had responded to their house. An ambulance was dispatched as well. The officer spoke with nineteen year old Brandon as the paramedics were preparing to transport him to the hospital. Within a couple of minutes the officer had a full confession from Brandon. He admitted to having stolen the car and to being the driver when I had tried to stop him. He would not rat out his friend, but the friend was the least of our concern.

The Evening Watch officer secured warrants on Brandon for Motor Vehicle Theft, to be served on him when he was released from the hospital. Since I now had all of his personal information, I took out charges on him for Fleeing and Attempting to Elude, Reckless Driving, Speeding, Suspended Driver's License, and just for good measure, No Tail Lights. The other officers on my shift were suitably impressed!

3

Coked Up Body Builder

In July of 1990, I responded as a backup unit with a female officer to a domestic call in a nice Lilburn neighborhood. When we got to the house, we discovered that the twenty year old girl had really been worked over. Both of her eyes were swollen. Her nose was bloody and her lip was busted. She was a mess! She told us that she lived at home with her parents who were out of town for the weekend. Lisa had invited her boyfriend to come over so that they could spend a romantic weekend together. Things did not turn out so well.

Lisa told us that her boyfriend, Jeff, was snorting cocaine Friday night and all day Saturday. Lisa knew that her parents would not approve of Jeff spending the weekend. She was also tired of his drug use, so she told him on Saturday night that he had to leave. He had gone into a rage and beaten her up and trashed some of the furniture in her parent's house. Jeff had left just before we arrived. Lisa kept saying, "I know that after you guys leave, he is going to come back and beat me again."

As Officer Kathy was getting all of the information for her report, I told them that I would go drive around the neighborhood and see if by chance Jeff was lurking nearby. Lisa told me that Jeff drove a white Ford Mustang. I asked her what he looked like.

She answered, "He's really big. He looks like a body builder. I'm pretty sure he is still using steroids."

That is great, I thought. *I am about to go one-on-one with Arnold Schwarzenegger! I doubt he is still around, though. He has to know that we are going to be looking for him.*

The neighborhood was fairly large. I checked all of the other streets and then saw the recreation area. They had a neighborhood swimming pool, tennis courts, and a playground for the kids. It was almost midnight and the recreation area was closed. The parking lot was dark as I drove through it. My headlights picked up a car on the far side of the parking lot. It was a white Mustang.

I attempted to advise dispatch that I would be out on our suspect. There was no response from radio. I keyed up again and got nothing. At that time there were a number of places throughout the county that were considered "dead spots" where there was no radio reception. I had just found one. I was already up to the Mustang in my police car, so I lit it up with my bright headlights, my takedown lights and my spotlight. I could see a white male sitting in the driver's seat. This was kind of a bad situation. No one knew I was out on the suspect. According to the police tactics manual, I should have backed off until I could make contact with dispatch or another officer to let someone know where I was. The problem was that if I left, Jeff would probably leave too. I did not want to have it on my conscience that I had allowed him to get away.

Before I could get out of my police car, Jeff was already out of the Mustang. In theory, officers usually want violators to stay in their vehicle. That gives the police a little more control of the situation. When Jeff walked around the car to where I could see him, I thought, *It is Arnold Schwarzenegger! That guy is huge and he looks pissed!*

I was out of my car quickly and I said, "Sir, would you please have a seat back in your car?"

"What do you want?" he asked. "I wasn't doing anything wrong."

"Sir, I really need you to have a seat in your car. I need to talk to you about something," I said.

"Is this about Lisa?" he asked. "We just had a little disagreement. Everything is fine. There is no need for the police to get involved."

"Jeff, it's a lot more serious than that and you know it," I said. I had not approached him yet. There were about fifteen feet between us. I could see that his eyes had that glazed over look of someone who had just done coke.

"Are you going to take me to jail?" Jeff asked.

Well, I thought, *yes I am but it would be nice to have about three or four more officers with me.* "Jeff, right now, I just want to get your side of the story. Why don't you tell me what happened?" I said, trying to stall for time. I keyed my radio up and transmitted my location again, hoping that maybe someone could hear me.

Jeff had had enough conversation. He said, "I don't have to tell you anything, and I am not going to jail." With that he started for his car.

I got to him just as he was opening the driver's door. I grabbed his right arm and thought I had grabbed an iron rod. He was so big and solid. I did have him off balance, though, and holding his arm in an arm bar, I spun to the right in a circle and slammed him down on the pavement of the parking lot. He landed hard but was immediately scrambling to his feet.

Jeff threw a straight right at my head that I was able to evade. It would probably have knocked me out if it had landed. I did not want to slug it out with this monster, so I stepped in and tried to sweep his feet out from under him. No luck. His legs were like tree trunks. It was time for Plan B. I snapped a quick kick into the groin. It landed solidly and I heard Jeff gasp. He was still standing, however, so I stepped in and threw a knee into the groin. I stepped back and pulled Jeff down to the pavement again. I managed to get one hand cuffed as he started to recover. He began trying to throw me off. I pulled the left hand that I had handcuffed upward behind his back. "Jeff, stop fighting or I am going to rip this shoulder out of the socket," I told him. "Give me your right hand!"

I increased the tension on his left shoulder by pulling the handcuffed hand upward. Jeff screamed in pain and finally gave me his right hand. As I was getting him handcuffed, Officer Kathy and another officer came squealing into the parking lot. My last transmission had gotten out on the radio. They helped me get Jeff searched and secured in my police car.

We decided that I would transport Jeff to the jail since I would be getting a Resisting Arrest warrant on him. I would also get the warrants on him for Battery on Lisa and Criminal Damage to Property for tearing up her parent's house. Kathy would complete the incident report and I would write a short supplemental report about my encounter with Jeff.

When we got to the jail, I told the deputies in book-in that Jeff was violent and was probably under the influence of cocaine. There were two deputies in book-in, a portly male and a tiny female. The male deputy squinted at Jeff and said, "He don't look too violent to me. You aren't going to give me any trouble, are ya boy?"

Jeff just looked at the deputy without answering. The male deputy searched him and then took the handcuffs off. As soon as the handcuffs were off, Jeff went crazy again. He grabbed the male deputy by the collar with his left hand and the female's collar with his right and starting swinging them around. It was kind of eerie. Jeff was not saying anything. He just seemed intent on slamming these two deputies into the wall.

I was amazed by how strong this guy was. He was literally lifting both of these deputies up on their toes and off the ground. Still holding them by their collars, he slammed the female into the wall before I could intervene. I quickly stepped in and hit Jeff just as hard as I could in the solar plexus. His legs quit working and he collapsed to the floor gasping and releasing the deputies. Neither one of them was seriously hurt. Several other deputies had witnessed this encounter from down the hall and had come running. They were thoroughly offended that someone would attempt to harm one of their own, even if that one of their own was not real bright. I stepped back as the crowd of deputies dragged Jeff into an empty cell. *Sometimes the wheels of justice turn slowly*, I thought, *and other times they move pretty quickly!*

4

Inclimate Weather and Idiots

I HAVE LIVED IN Georgia for most of my life. Georgia has interesting weather patterns that have caused me great stress as a police officer over the years. During the winter especially, our weather seems to bring out the deficiencies in people's ability to drive. We do not get much snow in the south but we do get plenty of ice. It is normal to have one or two ice storms a year. These have the effect of creating mass chaos throughout the state. Imagine what would happen if you put a hundred people in a hockey rink in street shoes and then told them that they all had to go from one end of the ice rink and back as fast as they could without falling down. Tell them that the fastest time would win a Varsity Chilli Dog. That is pretty much what happens on Atlanta's roads every time they ice over. You will see people driving at the same speed that they would drive if there was no ice on the roads. It is common to see cars start sliding on the ice and end up in the median. Or start sliding on the ice and hit a parked car. Or start sliding on the ice and hit the guard rail. Or slide off the road and then get hit by another sliding car. You get the picture. The only difference is that no one wins the chilli dog.

The state Department of Transportation and the local counties have vehicles to salt the roads and de-ice them. But remember this is the south and we don't have the fleets of salt trucks that they have up north or out west. This means that the interstates get treated, as well as the main surface streets, but that is all until the police request them to a specific location in suburbia.

A number of years ago, I was working the overnight shift during an ice storm. The first part of my shift was pretty crazy and everybody stayed busy working car wrecks. After a while, the traffic died down and we were able to catch up on our reports. The temperatures dropped well below freezing again and the freezing rain continued throughout the night. About five thirty in the morning, traffic began to pick up as people started for work. The DOT crews had treated the main roads and many of the other surface streets throughout the night, but there was no way that they could get to them all. The vehicle accident calls started coming in. It was going to be a long morning.

Radio dispatched me to an accident just south of Lawrenceville. The dispatcher said that a car had slid off the road and into a ditch. When I got there, I was cautious as I approached. I slowed the police car down to a crawl. I did not want to become another casualty of the ice. Before I realized it, though, I was sliding on a patch of ice that was several hundred feet long. Thankfully, I was going slow enough not to lose control. I stopped the police car, activated the blue lights, and turned the car sideways, blocking the road. The Toyota Corolla was in the ditch just a short walk from where I stopped. The road was very slippery and it was all I could do to stay on my feet. I managed to get to the car without falling. The woman who was driving was shaken up but not hurt. She was very fortunate in that her Corolla wasn't damaged. She just needed a tow truck to get her out of the ditch.

I requested another police car to block the road in the other direction so we would not have any more wrecks and a salt truck to come and treat the road. There were no other officers available, however, because they were all dealing with car accidents of their own. Dispatch told me that they would give my request for a salt truck to the DOT. While we were waiting on a tow truck, I let the woman sit in the back of my patrol car out of the cold. The temperature was nineteen degrees. I had just about gotten some feeling back in my hands when I saw a car coming down the road. One would think that the blue lights might have made the driver slow down or even stop to see what was going on. Instead, this guy, in his Chevrolet S-10 pickup truck, just kept coming. When he hit the ice, the truck started sliding. He slid past me, spun around a couple of times, and slammed hard into the ditch just up from the first lady's car.

Leaving the woman in my warm police car, I slid and stumbled over to where the pickup was in the ditch. Other than a knot on his head, the driver was okay. He refused my offer of an ambulance. His truck, however, needed some serious help. The front end and driver's side was really banged up. The left front tire was flat and it looked like he had bent his front axle. I requested another tow truck for the smashed up S-10.

"I didn't know the road was so icy," the driver said.

"The police car across the road with its blue lights on should have clued you in. That and the fact that it sleeted all night," I replied.

"Oh, I saw the police car," the not so bright gentleman said. "I didn't know it meant that I should stop."

"How did that work out for you?" I asked, pointing at his smashed pickup. I turned around and shuffled back to my police car to write up an accident report for the S-10. I pointedly left the driver standing in the cold to wait on his tow truck. There is something about stupidity that just drains the compassion out of me. I was almost back to my warm cruiser when I saw another car coming from the opposite direction. This driver slowed down at the sight of the blue lights but did not stop. By the time she realized that she needed to stop, her Ford Taurus was on the ice and sliding. Not only was she sliding, she was sliding directly towards my police car. At the last moment, the Taurus somehow slid around my police car and spun off the road into a shallow part of the ditch behind the first car. This lady had at least slowed down so the damage to her car was very minimal.

As I was slipping and sliding over to check on her, I was seriously questioning my career choice. *This is not what I imagined when I became a police officer*, I thought. These thoughts were reinforced as I saw another car coming from the same direction. This was a big car and it wasn't slowing down. It turned out to be a Cadillac and as soon as it hit the ice, it started spinning out of control. Thankfully, it missed the police car and came to a stop in the yard on the other side of the road, just missing a large tree.

I still needed to check on the lady in the Taurus. I also needed to get the woman out of my police car because of the two near misses. Moving the police car was kind of out of the question. There really wasn't any safe place to put it because cars were sliding off the road in both directions. Then I needed to check on the driver in the Cadillac. The driver from the S-10 was still shivering, waiting on his tow truck. I radioed dispatch again, alerting her that I now multiple accidents and really needed some help. Lieutenant Wally was probably in his warm office drinking coffee, but he heard the distress in my voice and said he was on his way to help me.

The lady in the Ford Taurus was fine. She had at least slowed down enough so that she had not hit anything. She had just slid out off the road. There was no damage to her car but she would need to be pulled out of the ditch. I told her that there were already tow trucks coming and we would get her out of the ditch. She apologized, "I slowed down when I saw the blue lights, but then when I tried to stop, I was on the ice and it was too late."

I left her with her car and managed to get back to the police car without falling down. I told the lady in my backseat that she had to get out because of the likelihood that the police car was going to get hit. I directed her over to the front yard where the Cadillac was. It was a big yard so it would probably be safe there if she got far enough away from the road.

The older woman in the Cadillac was shaken up but unhurt. She had not hit anything but her car was stuck in the mud and ice. The wrecker drivers were going to earn their money today, if they ever arrived. The Cadillac driver said, "I didn't know the road was so icy. Why wasn't someone stopping traffic?"

"Lady, there is a police car blocking the street with its blue lights on, there are three cars in the ditch, and it sleeted all night. What more did you need? You should have been going slower. Be grateful that you did not hurt someone with your poor driving."

This got her attention. She said, "I'll have you know I am a very good driver."

I laughed and said, "So, that is why you are in the middle of these people's front yard?"

The people, whose front yard that we were in, had been awakened by the chaos in front of their house. Mr and Mrs Johnson came outside to see what was going on. Mrs Johnson invited all the stranded drivers into their house to get warm. Mr Johnson put on a pot of coffee. Lieutenant Wally showed up and used his police car to block the other end of the road. From what I had seen so far, though, this was no guarantee that we were done with the madness. The wreckers still had not gotten there. I figured that they were either on other accident calls or delayed by the weather conditions.

Lieutenant Wally had just blocked off his section of the road, when a truck came flying down the road on my side. The driver must have seen the blue lights because the Ford F-150 started slowing. The vehicle was slowing down but then was on the ice and sliding. The driver was really fighting to control the truck. The black pickup spun around a couple of times and then stopped in the middle of the road, about ten feet from my police car. I realized that I had been holding my breath and exhaled. I started walking across the Johnson's front yard to congratulate the driver of the F-150 on not hitting the police cruiser when I saw more headlights coming from the same direction. The minivan wasn't going that fast but it wasn't stopping. When it hit the ice, it slid in a straight line and crashed into the F-150. This sent the F-150 sliding right into my patrol car. The pickup truck took the brunt of the hit so that when it crashed into the left rear quarter panel of the police car, it was only going a few miles an hour. The police car was damaged, but it could have been a lot worse. The Chevrolet Astrovan that hit the F-150, however, was really messed up. The front end was smashed and it was not going to be driven away. The pickup truck had some body damage but it would not have to be towed. Neither driver was hurt.

Fortunately, the salt truck and the first wrecker arrived and we were able to start getting things cleaned up. I only had to write two accident reports, one for the S-10 in the ditch and one for the Astrovan, the F-150, and the police car. The other cars weren't damaged. They just needed to be pulled back onto the road. I issued a citation to the driver of the S-10 and one to the driver of the Astrovan for Too Fast for Conditions. Hopefully, all of these people learned a thing or two about driving on the ice but I doubt it.

5

Drunk Drivers

One of things that police officers face on a daily or nightly basis are impaired drivers. That is the politically correct term for drunk drivers. It goes without saying that drunk drivers kill hundreds or possibly even thousands of innocent people every year in the United States. While the penalties for Driving Under the Influence in Georgia and nationwide have become much more severe, it has also become much more difficult for police officers to make DUI cases. For sure, even a first offense DUI conviction carries a mandatory driver's license suspension, mandatory jail time, and hefty fines. At the same time, many defense attorneys make a fortune by representing people charged with DUI. These defense attorneys have lobbied State Legislatures all over the country to include certain loopholes in much of the current DUI Law.

It is not uncommon to see good DUI cases reduced to Reckless Driving in a negotiated plea bargain when the case goes to trial. For the defendant, this is well worth the ten thousand dollars or more that they are paying their attorney to negotiate the deal. It allows the defendant to keep their driver's license, reduces the amount of their fines, and negates possible jail time. I have seen other good DUI cases thrown out because the officer failed to follow some minor procedural issue that had little bearing on the case.

I was in court several years ago and saw this happen. A young officer had arrested a man for Speeding and DUI. The drunk had registered a .15 grams on the breath test. That is basically double the legal limit of .08 grams. When we arrest someone for Driving Under the Influence, we are required to read them their "Implied Consent Warning." This is read off of a card that we keep in our pocket and advises the person that they are required to submit to a state administered test to determine if they are under the influence of alcohol or drugs. It also lets them know that their driver's license will be suspended if they refuse to take the test. Every few years, Implied Consent Law is changed and the cards we have to read off of are updated as well. In the case above, this had just happened but the young officer had read off of the wrong card. The law had not changed that much but because he had read off of the "old" card, the DUI charge was thrown out. The guy paid a fine for the speeding charge and walked out of court jubilant. He probably stopped for a drink or three on his way home. Is it any wonder that drunk drivers kill so many people every year? OK, I will get off of my soapbox now. This chapter will contain some of the more interesting DUI cases that I made during my law enforcement career.

One night, about two in the morning, I was on patrol in the Norcross area. I got behind a white 300 Series Mercedes Benz. What got my attention was the fact that the car was straddling the line separating the two Northbound lanes on Holcomb Bridge Road. Other traffic was backing up because no one could get around the Mercedes that was taking up both lanes. When I got behind it, I activated my blue lights and advised the dispatcher of my traffic stop. The Mercedes did not speed up or slow down. It just kept going, still straddling the line. I turned on my siren and shone my spotlight in the vehicle's rear view mirror. Finally, after almost a mile, the Mercedes pulled over near the Chattahoochee River, at the Gwinnett/Fulton county lines.

As I walked up to the car, I saw that the driver was a female and the only person in the car. When she looked over at me, I knew right away that she was intoxicated. Her eyes were completely glazed over and she could not focus. The odor of booze was really strong coming out of her window. I saw that the gear shift lever was still in the "Drive" position. If her foot slipped off the brake, we were going to have problems. I said, "Hey, Ma'am, can you please put your car in "Park?"

She appeared to not have heard me. She was fumbling around with her purse as if she was looking for her driver's license. I asked her again to put the car in "Park." This time she nodded and turned her turn signal on. *Wow*! I thought, *She is really Drunk!* She was finally able get the gear shift lever to "Park."

I asked the woman for her driver's license. She handed me a credit card. *I see a holding cell in your future*, I thought. "Where are you heading tonight, Ma'am?" I asked.

"Grayson," She answered. I was stunned. Grayson was on the other side of the county, about twenty five miles away. She was driving in the opposite direction to where she wanted to go. She had no clue where she was or even what road she was on.

Even though it was very clear that this driver was intoxicated, I still had to try and have her perform some Field Sobriety Tests. These tests are part of what it takes to build a good DUI case. "Ma'am, would you please step out of the car?"

The blond, fairly attractive, drunk woman stepped out of the car. She was wearing a white dress and high heels. I had to grab her arm because she staggered out into a lane of traffic. I guided her to the rear of my patrol car and out of the road. Field Sobriety Tests are designed to test the basic reflexes and coordination of the possibly impaired driver. These tests all have an element that divides the person's attention. An intoxicated person has real difficulty focusing on more than one thing at a time.

I asked the woman, Michelle, if she would take some sobriety tests for me. She said, "Sure," and then stumbled and fell backwards against the police car. At that point, I went ahead and told her she was under arrest and handcuffed her. If she couldn't even stand up, I wasn't about to try and give her sobriety tests. She might fall down and hurt herself.

While I was waiting on the wrecker that was coming to impound Michelle's Mercedes Benz, I heard her talking in the back. "What is that smell?" she asked. I could not smell anything with the plexiglass screen between us. When the wrecker got there, I got out and had him sign the impound sheet. When I got back in my police car, Michelle said, "Somebody spilled something on me."

One of the things about drunk people is that they often ramble and say stuff that does not make any sense. Michelle continued to insist that someone had poured something on her. Well, she was the only one in the back seat so I really did not pay any attention to what she was saying. I turned some music on and tried to tune her out as we drove to the jail.

When we got to the jail, I opened the back door of the police car for Michelle to get out. As she was sliding out she said again, "Something smells. I think someone spilled something on me."

When she got out of the car, I finally understood what she was talking about. Her white dress had turned yellow around her crotch. She had urinated on herself and didn't even realize it. I got her into the jail and she took a breath-a-lyzer test. She registered .25 grams. That would mean unconsciousness for most people, yet this woman was trying to drive. The deputies gave her an orange jumpsuit to change into until she bonded out.

Another night, I got behind a large black Cadillac Eldorado near Buford. This was one of those cars that was about half a block long. It was driving shoulder to shoulder on that particular two lane stretch of Peachtree Industrial Boulevard. Thankfully, there was no other traffic on the road. The Eldorado was speeding up and slowing down as it weaved all over the road.

When my blue lights came on, the car accelerated like it was going to run, but then, just as suddenly, the driver slammed on the brakes and skidded to a stop in the middle of the road. The driver was a middle-aged black guy. I could smell the alcohol as I walked up to the open driver's window. Leon was a very personable drunk. I asked him where he was going.

"Well, you see, Officer, I was at my girlfriend's house. Now, I am trying to get home before my wife finds out that I was gone."

"I can smell the booze, sir. How many beers have you had tonight?" I asked.

Leon turned his nose up and looked offended. "I don't drink beer, Officer. I only drink bourbon. I have had a few sips tonight."

Leon agreed to take some Field Sobriety Tests. He failed all of them but he was not as bad as some impaired drivers that I had seen. When he took the breath test at the jail, though, the results indicated that he was at .29 grams. This is over three times the legal limit. Talking to Leon, he did not seem that drunk. His driving, however, and the sobriety tests were the indicators that he was intoxicated. He was evidently a serious drinker to be able to function at .29 grams. I do not know whether or not Leon's wife ever found out about his girlfriend or if his girlfriend ever found out about his wife.

Another time, one of my academy mates, Corporal Robert, and I were sitting side by side in our police cars late one night at the very end of a large strip shopping center. We were drinking coffee and catching up on our paperwork. I was a Corporal at the time as well, but that night,

I was the Acting Sergeant for my shift. The shopping center was mostly empty. All of the businesses were closed except for the bar on the far end. This was a Wednesday night/Thursday morning so there were only a few cars parked in front of the bar.

We had been sitting there for about half an hour when the world exploded. At least that was what it sounded like. The noise was so loud, so sudden, and so unexpected that Robert and I instinctively reacted by putting our police cars in drive and pulling away. We thought that we were being shot at and we both were trying to get out of the kill zone. We are lucky that we did not slam our cruisers into each other. As we were accelerating out of the way, I saw what had caused the loud explosion sound.

My headlights picked up a white work van with a ladder rack on it that had just ran head on into a dumpster about fifty feet from where we were sitting. As my headlights illuminated the scene, the driver of the van backed up about twenty feet and then gunned the van forward again, striking the dumpster a second time. The noise of the van slamming into the large, empty, metallic dumpster echoed throughout the parking lot. The van had come from behind the dark shopping center and was driving without having its headlights on.

Robert and I activated our blue lights and quickly pulled over to the van. We approached the driver with our pistols drawn. As we got to the driver's door, I could see that the Hispanic male was intoxicated. His eyes were glazed over and his movements were slow. Corporal Robert quickly opened the door and pulled the guy out before he could try and drive away.

It turned out that the guy was an illegal Mexican construction worker. He had been at the bar at the far end of the shopping center and was on his way home. He had just forgotten to turn his headlights on. When he rounded the corner of the shopping center and saw the two police cars sitting there, he got a little distracted and ran into the dumpster. Why he backed up and then slammed into it again is a mystery known only to him.

Corporal Robert has Puerto Rican roots and speaks Spanish fluently. The drunk Mexican told him that he did not have a driver's license and that he had had, "a few beers at the bar." I'm not really sure how many, "a few," was but this guy was really drunk. He could barely stand without having to lean against his van. Robert did not even bother to give him Field Sobriety Tests. If you are so drunk that you can't stand up, that automatically earns you a trip to the jail.

One night, I had stopped in at a convenience store on Highway 78, just outside of Snellville. It was early in the shift but I felt the need for some coffee. I had fixed my coffee and was chatting with the clerk, Salah, when the front door opened and a man stumbled into the store. He was a white guy in his fifties. He swayed and stumbled to the back of the store. He grabbed a carton of chocolate milk and came to the front to pay for it. He nodded at me but didn't say anything. I could see that his movements were unsteady and he reeked of alcohol. *There is no way this guy is driving*, I thought. *Someone must have given him a ride to the store.* It was difficult for him to even get money out of his wallet. He finally managed to pay for his chocolate milk, nodded at me again, and then stumbled out of the store.

Salah said, "He is in here every night. He stops in on his way home from the bar across the street."

"You mean he is driving?" I asked.

"Oh yes. He always parks on the side of the building."

I thanked Salah and left the store. I saw the drunk leaving the parking lot in a brown pickup truck, without any lights on. I caught up to him about a half mile down the road. The guy still had not turned his headlights on and it was almost one in the morning. I turned on my blue lights and got the pickup truck stopped. He was another one that was too drunk for Field Sobriety tests. His driver's license was already suspended for a previous Driving Under the Influence arrest. He blew a .28 grams when he was tested at the jail. I asked the guy if he had seen me in the convenience store. He just shrugged and said, "I did but I didn't think I was that bad."

One of my favorite DUI arrests came off of Interstate 85. I got behind a speeding pickup truck one night that was weaving all over the expressway. It was about three o'clock in the morning so there wasn't that much traffic on the road. This section of I-85 had four northbound lanes at the time and this pickup truck was using all of them. The truck was going about fifteen miles over the speed limit but could not stay in a single lane.

I could only see the driver in the truck. I advised dispatch of the pullover and turned on my blue lights. As soon as the blue lights came on, I saw a head pop up from the driver's lap and slide over into the passenger seat. The truck pulled over onto the shoulder and stopped. When I walked up to the driver's door, I could see that the driver, a big white guy had his pants undone and his private parts sticking out. The passenger was also a white guy. The passenger had evidently been entertaining the driver in a very special way as they were driving.

That is not something you see every day, I thought. I could smell the alcohol coming out of the window. I got the driver's license and had him step out of the truck. He was hurriedly trying to stuff himself back into his jeans as he got out of his vehicle. The problem with being drunk, however, is that it really messes with your coordination and he could not get his pants snapped for anything. He was big rugged guy. His name was Joe and he was a General Contractor. He had built subdivisions all over the area. He admitted to having been drinking. He said that he had been at a bar in downtown Atlanta and was heading to his suburban home. His "friend," was a guy he had met at the bar. He could not recall his name.

Joe told me that he had had several drinks earlier in the evening. He said he would submit to some Field Sobriety Tests. The first one was a simple recitation of the alphabet. I had him stand up straight with his feet together and then told him to begin. He omitted several letters and transposed a few more. Strike One.

Next, I had him to extend his arms straight out to his sides, tilt his head back, and then close his eyes. At my instruction, he had to simply take the index finger that I specified and touch the tip of his nose. He was already starting to sway before I even told him which arm to use. I told him to use his left index finger. He used his right one and missed the tip of his nose. I gave him another chance to use his left index finger and he missed with that one as well. Strike Two.

The last test that I used was that I asked Joe to count backwards from fifty until I told him to stop. I again had him stand up straight with his feet together and told him to begin. He got to forty five and then started skipping numbers and even repeating a few. Strike Three. I told him that he was under arrest for Driving Under the Influence and handcuffed him.

After I got him in the police car, I went and talked to the passenger. His name was Donnie and he was very sweet, in an effeminate sort of way. He was also very intoxicated as well. He lived in downtown Atlanta. I requested another officer to join me at the scene to take Donnie to a payphone so he could call someone to come and get him. This was before the days when everyone had a cell phone. When the other officer arrived, he did a cursory pat down of Donnie before he put him in the police car. No one gets a ride from the police without being checked to make sure that they are unarmed. Donnie really seemed to enjoy the pat down.

After they had left, I did an inventory of Joe's truck. I had already called for a wrecker to impound it. As I was looking through it, I found several items of artwork from a young child. I asked Joe about the artwork. If he was gay, it seemed a bit out of place for him to have some child's artwork with him. He said, "Those are my children. My wife and I are going through a divorce. She won't let me see my kids. It is killing me!" He started crying.

When I got Joe to the jail, he registered .13 grams on the breath test. I was still a fairly new police officer. When I wrote the arrest report, I left out the part about Donnie and what he was doing to Joe as they were driving. I felt sorry for the guy and did not want to embarrass him. I had made a good DUI arrest so I knew that this case would never go to court. I just mentioned the speeding and the weaving in my report as the reasons for the stop and then discussed the Field Sobriety Tests.

I was surprised a few months later when I received a subpoena to go to court and testify in Joe's DUI trial. This was on one of my off days and I was a bit perturbed. When I got to court, I saw that Joe had hired him a high dollar attorney to represent him. The attorney sauntered over to me before the judge came in and asked me if he could talk to me about the case. Usually, I would have told him to save his questions for when I was on the stand. However, I really did not want to be there any longer than I had to be on an off day. Maybe by talking to this lawyer before the trial, I could speed the process up.

I asked the lawyer what he wanted to know. I could see Joe sitting on the other side of the courtroom in an expensive suit, looking like a serious businessman who really should not be found guilty of these trumped up charges. The attorney started off by saying in a very condescending tone, "You know he only blew .13 grams. This isn't a really good case. How about if we drop the DUI charge and just let him plead to Reckless Driving?"

The lawyer must have thought that because I was young, I was also stupid. I laughed at Mr. Attorney and said, "No way. I really want the jury to hear about this arrest. I think they will enjoy this story. Did your client tell you about his friend that he had with him when I arrested him…the one that he had picked up at a gay bar in Atlanta?"

Mr. Attorney's face went pale and he pulled out a copy of my arrest report and quickly scanned it. He said, "There is nothing in your report about that."

"No, there isn't," I answered. "I saw no need to embarrass your client when I arrested him. Since he wants a trial, though, I am sure the jury would enjoy hearing what Joe's new boyfriend was doing to him while your client was driving drunk. I am going to tell the jury that your client's pants were undone, his privates were sticking out, and his new best friend Donnie's head was in his lap. I think the judge might even get a chuckle out of that one. Joe's ex-wife will probably want a copy of the transcript of my testimony, too."

I saw perspiration beading on the lawyer's forehead. I think he felt like a man who had just picked up a rattlesnake by the tail. He wanted to drop it and get away from it as quickly as he could. He said, "Uh, can you excuse me for a moment? I need to talk to my client."

Mr. Attorney walked across the courtroom and put his mouth to Joe's ear. In a few seconds, the color had drained from Joe's face and he glared over at me. I winked at him and smiled. Joe said something to his lawyer and then walked out of the courtroom.

The lawyer slowly walked back over to me. He chuckled nervously and said, "In light of these new, uh, developments, my client has decided that he would like to just go ahead and plead guilty to these charges and put this behind him."

"That is too bad," I said. "I was really looking forward to telling that story to the jury!"

Joe's lawyer was there with him when he plead guilty to Driving Under the Influence. Joe lost his driver's license for a year, paid fifteen hundred dollars in fines, and was on probation for twelve months. I learned my lesson on that arrest. Never omit pertinent facts from a report. Write a thorough, comprehensive report the first time. When an officer writes a good report, it is much less likely that they will have to go to court and waste a perfectly good off day.

6

Training, Training, Training

In *Street Cop*, I included a chapter about the whole Police Academy experience. Our Training Division does an excellent job of equipping someone to do their job as a police officer. After the academy's formal four months of training, the Field Training Officers then have the responsibility to mold the young recruits into effective crime fighting machines. The FTO's teach the recruits how to apply what they learned in the classroom to real life situations. To be an FTO, officers are required to complete an intense week long course. I was a Field Training Officer for many years.

When a recruit graduates from the Police Academy, their classroom training has not ended, either. Like any other profession, Law Enforcement requires continuous training. Laws change every year. Court rulings, such as a Supreme Court decision, affect how various laws are enforced. New technologies require new training. Even lawsuits affect how police departments train their officers.

Here is a breakdown of how officers are continually being trained at my department. The State of Georgia requires law enforcement officers to receive twenty hours of training every year to maintain their certification. This equates to two full days of training at some point during the year plus a quarterly qualification with our pistols. The two days of training might include legal or policy updates, drivers training, defensive tactics and impact weapons training, a first aid/CPR refresher, and many other topics.

In addition to the required training that everyone has to attend, supervisors and managers usually have at least one in-service class during the year related to management and Human Resource issues. Officers may also request to attend optional classes that are offered throughout the year. Some of these optional courses include Taser training, a patrol rifle course, Advanced Defensive Tactics, Crime Scene Processing, and Spanish for Police Officers. They can request to take training at our Training Center or at one of the other state police academies.

Another place that officers receive on-going training is in their roll calls at the various precincts. Sergeants conduct the fifteen minute roll call prior to each shift. Several times a week, five or ten minutes will be devoted to some aspect of training. While five or ten minutes may not sound like much, these are some of the most effective training sessions that officers will receive. Typically, these roll call training topics will have arisen from a call or incident that officers have dealt with in last day or two. It will be something that is fresh in everybody's mind and a good opportunity to reinforce proper procedures and tactics. Roll call training often includes short video clips that the Sergeant or Lieutenant have found on the news or on the internet of an officer displaying correct or incorrect tactics. Videos are a great teaching aid and usually generate lively discussion.

I have had the opportunity over the last thirty years to attend a variety of different police schools. I have taken classes at my own police academy, as well as travelling and taking courses at the state police academy. The Georgia Police Academy is about an hour south of Atlanta. I have been there numerous times for a variety of different types of training. The rest of the chapter will provide a couple of examples of those classes, the Good, the Bad, and the Ugly.

One of the most enjoyable weeks of training that I ever had was at the Georgia Police Academy. The course was called, "Wilderness Crimes Investigation." I had turned in the school request not really expecting to get approved to go. My Lieutenant at the time, Lieutenant Wally, asked me why I wanted to take the training. I reminded him that a majority of our county was still rural and it was not uncommon to have to track criminals into the woods. At that time, in the late 1980's, we also did not have the number of tracking canines that we do today.

I figured Lieutenant Wally was going to tell me, "No," and that would be the end of it. Instead, he said, "That sounds like a good time. I think I am going to go with you."

The Lieutenant and I were in our places in the classroom on the first day of the course. The first two days were spent teaching us how to use a compass and a map. This was before handheld GPS's had hit the market. After lunch on the second day, we were in the woods of South Georgia, going from point to point, using our compasses and maps to find our way through the woods.

On the third day, we were given a training scenario. We were told that there was an illegal whiskey still somewhere on the two thousand acres surrounding the police academy. We were put into teams of three or four people. Our first mission was to locate the still without being detected. After we had completed the first mission, we were to withdraw back to the classroom. There, all the teams would work together to develop a tactical plan to go back to the still after dark and arrest anyone who we found there.

My team was composed of Lieutenant Wally, me, and Bill, a middle aged officer from a small department in South Georgia. We don't have many illegal whiskey stills where I police and this was something that Lieutenant Wally and I were not really familiar with. However, I did know that to make good whiskey, or any whiskey for that matter, you had to have a water source. Each group was huddled around their map discussing where they should go look. We had been told that the first group to locate the still would be in charge of the takedown and arrest operation later. Plus, they would have bragging rights.

As we huddled around our map, I had heard some of the other group's conversations. I had not heard anyone mention the need for a water source. They were just looking at the maps and trying to imagine a good location to put a still. I spoke quietly to Lieutenant Wally and Bill, "I think we need to concentrate on the creek."

I explained what I was thinking and their eyes lit up. "Spell, I think you are onto something," the Lieutenant said.

I pointed out several areas that looked likely. I figured that if you were making illegal whiskey, you would want to be down in a valley or hollow to avoid detection. According to the map, there were several of those. While the other groups were still looking at their maps and discussing options, our group headed out into the woods to see what we could find.

The first hollow that we checked was empty. The second one was several hundred yards away through the woods. We approached it very quietly and took it under observation from about one hundred yards away. Bingo! We lay on the edge of an embankment, hidden by the brush. We passed the binoculars around. We could see the fifty gallon wooden barrels, the pipes, the various containers, and other components of the still. The still was nestled under a steep embankment about twenty feet from the creek. There was no one around it. While we knew that this was just a training exercise, it still gave us a rush to be the ones to make the discovery. We marked the location on our maps and backed out quietly.

When we got back to the classroom, we saw that we were the first group to get back. The instructor was amazed at how quickly we had found the still. Yep, we had the bragging rights. When the other five groups got back, all but two teams had also eventually located the still.

While our group was going to lead the tactical part of the mission, I knew that I was the junior man. Lieutenant Wally was the ranking officer, and Bill was a Corporal at his department. At the time, I was just a patrolman. This would be the Lieutenant's briefing. Lieutenant Wally had other plans. He told me, "This is your show. I want you to run the briefing and planning session. It was your good idea that led us to the still. You can lead us in taking it down."

Having seen the terrain surrounding the still, I had a general idea of what we needed to do. My team and one other would be the actual assault team. The other four teams would be placed strategically around the location to prevent anyone from escaping. I drew it up on a chalkboard and we discussed the approach routes that each group would take. After everyone was sure of their responsibilities, we started for the location. It was nice and dark and there was not much of a moon. The plan called for each team being in place and watching the still for at least an hour, waiting to see if anyone showed up.

We had walkie-talkies and each team checked in, letting me know that they were in place. After about twenty minutes, an officer whispered that they had movement near them on the trail, heading towards the still. He said it looked like two subjects with flashlights. A minute later, we saw them approaching the still. I gave the order to move in and the takedown team moved in yelling, "Police! Get down on the ground!"

One of the subjects complied immediately and dropped to his knees. The other guy tried to run and one of the groups on the perimeter scooped him up and brought him back to the still. The two "suspects," were police academy instructors, recruited to be role players. They were wearing coveralls, work boots, and each had a ball cap on. They really looked the part. They could not get over how smoothly the operation had gone. The instructor who had tried to run away said that our team was the first one that had ever caught him. He said that, usually, once he got into the shadows, away from the still, he was gone.

The last big exercise that we had in our "Wilderness Crimes Investigation" course was a tough one. Our instructions were pretty simple. We were given a map and a set of coordinates. We were told that we were being dropped off in the middle of the thirty five thousand acre Piedmont National Forest and that we had to locate the coordinates on the map. At that location, we would find a marijuana grow operation. Our mission was to take it under surveillance without being spotted. We were to gather as much intelligence as we could and then withdraw to another set of coordinates.

We were still in our same teams. Each group was dropped off at a different location, but everyone was about the same distance away from the target. Lieutenant Wally, Bill, and I headed into the woods, holding our map and a compass. We knew we were in trouble when the small "creek" that the map indicated we had to cross, turned out to be a twenty foot wide, fast moving river. Of course, the coordinates that we were looking for were on the other side of the river. The river slowed us down for a while.

It was in the fall of the year and starting to get cold. Even if the Lieutenant and I had gone ahead and swam across, Bill was a good bit older and probably would not have made it. A few hundred yards downstream, we found a tree that had fallen across the river. It spanned almost the entire length. We just had to jump the last few feet to the opposite bank and none of us even got our feet wet.

We eventually got to a place where we could watch the area that we were supposed to watch. There was a guy walking in circles in the woods, acting like he was guarding his marijuana. When we had watched him for a while, we had to make our way to another set of coordinates that turned out to be a road, where a car was waiting for us to take us back to the Academy. To pass this exercise, all you had to do was report back what the guy we had seen had been wearing and to make sure that he had not seen us.

While this was probably one of the best courses that I ever attended, the State Police Academy also hosted one of the worst courses that I ever went to. I have been involved in some sort of Martial Art most of my life. I have trained in a variety of different systems. While I feel that I have maintained a level of proficiency in fighting and defensive tactics over the years, I am always willing to learn something new. When I saw that the State Police Academy was putting on a week long Advanced Defensive Tactics course, I asked to go. Lieutenant Wally signed off on the training request and I again headed to South Georgia.

I knew that it was going to be a long week when Betty White walked in on the first day of class and said that she was going to be our lead instructor for the week. In reality, she wasn't quite as old as Betty White, but I was not alone in thinking that someone's white-haired grandmother was going to try and teach us how to fight better.

Now I know that if this were a movie, Betty would have invited a volunteer from the audience and would have proceeded to whip his ass in front of the class to show that she was the real deal. It did not work out that way. Nope, she was just as inept as she looked.

When Betty did ask for a volunteer to demonstrate a technique on, it did not work out so well for her. She told us that she was going to show us how to break a front choke grip. When the male student put the choke on her, Betty almost passed out trying to get free. The student finally felt sorry for her and let her neck go. We tried not to snicker too loudly.

At some point, on the first day a student asked the instructor how long she had been teaching Defensive Tactics. She told us she had only been in her position for a year. She said that she had been the Chief of Police over the campus police department that took care of the State Police Academy. To save money, the department had been disbanded. The head of the police academy felt bad about Betty being out of a job so he asked her if she wanted to come teach at the police academy. He gave her a choice to teach anything that she wanted. She told us, "Defensive Tactics looked like fun so I became a Defensive Tactics Instructor."

The week was not a total loss for me. My workout partner for the week was Tyrone. He was an officer with a small department in South Georgia. Tyrone had played college football for Georgia Southern University. He was a defensive lineman until he blew his knee out his senior year. After college, he became a police officer. Tyrone was still a monster physically. He was about six foot four and weighed around two hundred and sixty pounds. He looked like he could still play football.

Since it was clear that Betty was in over her head, Tyrone and I worked together and had a good time throughout the week. At first he scoffed that any type of martial art would be effective against anyone of his size and strength. After I put him on his knees a few times using joint-locks, he became a believer and an eager learner. I taught him a few simple joint-locks and pressure points. He taught me quite a bit about the footwork, balance, and strategy needed to defeat a big blocker and how to handle it when you are being double teamed.

While on-going training is important to any profession, I think that in Law Enforcement, it is often the difference between life and death. Studies and real life situations have shown over and over that, in a crisis, we always fall back to the level of our training. If we have trained well, then we will respond well. If we haven't trained well, then the consequences could be tragic. Our Department has one of the best Training Divisions in the country. They consistently provide quality training, which in turn, has led to our Department having a reputation as one of the best police departments in the nation.

7

Accident on the Interstate

WE ALL HAVE MEMORIES of key events in our lives. There are some things that are so traumatic that they become permanently etched on our psyche. For me, one of those days was November 21, 1987. I was patrolling on the Day Shift and I got behind a large truck on Pleasant Hill Road near Duluth. I noticed that the license plate had been expired for almost a year. I notified the dispatcher that I was going to be on a traffic stop and turned on my blue lights. The truck was turning onto Interstate 85 Northbound and did not pull over until he had already merged onto the interstate. Traffic was heavy at eight thirty in the morning and he stopped as soon as he could.

The driver pulled over into the emergency lane of the interstate in response to my blue lights. I had him step out of the truck and spoke to him between our two vehicles, out of the traffic. He was an older white man. I told him why I had stopped him and pointed to the expired license plate. He said, "Officer, I am so sorry. I just started working for this company two days ago. This is a company vehicle and I had no idea the tag was expired."

Bob, the driver, gave me his driver's license and an identification card from the company that did show that he had just started working there. I told Bob that I was going to write him a warning ticket for the tag. He could take it in and show his boss. Hopefully, the company would get the license plate renewed immediately.

As I sat in my patrol car writing the warning citation, Bob stood on the shoulder. Fortunately for him, he was not standing between the two vehicles. He was off to the side a few feet. The last thing that I remembered was a loud crash and then seeing a bright flash. I found myself lying partially in the passenger seat. As I tried to sit up, I saw that the police car had been slammed into the back of the large truck that I had stopped. I noticed a small white car laying upside down in the middle of the interstate a few lanes from where we were.

As I struggled to get out on the passenger side of the police car, I saw Bob lying down on the shoulder. He was moaning and holding his face. I could see blood seeping out between his fingers. As I tried to stand up, I realized that my head was really hurting. I touched my forehead and felt a knot beginning to form. I looked at my police car and saw that it was mangled. It had been struck from behind and the 1986 Ford Crown Victoria was totaled.

I quickly went to check on Bob. He had some nasty cuts on his face caused by flying glass but nothing appeared to be life threatening. I called dispatch and advised that I had been involved in an accident with injuries. I told her that I was injured as well and requested an ambulance. Within just a few minutes, I could hear sirens coming my way.

I began to realize that the small white car that I had seen lying upside down was the one that had hit me. Somehow, he had swung over into the emergency lane and slammed into me, knocking my police car into the truck. The Chevette, as it turned out to be, then flipped over, coming to rest on its top in the middle of the interstate. The miracle was that no one ran into the Chevette, or hit the driver as he came crawling out. The Chevette's driver came stumbling out of the traffic. He was a white guy in his mid twenties. His face was bloody and he was limping.

The Chevette's driver, Timothy, looked at the carnage and then asked me, "What were you doing in my way, man?"

Fortunately, other officers had started to arrive. One saw me take a step towards Timothy and quickly intervened. He guided me away from Timothy and back to an ambulance that had just arrived. The paramedics quickly strapped me to a board and put a collar around my neck. My head was pounding and I could feel the lump throbbing on my forehead from being slammed into the windshield. My neck and back were hurting, and my right knee felt like it was starting to swell.

Bob and Timothy were also transported to the hospital. For whatever reason, we were all transported in the same ambulance. Timothy mumbled and talked the entire way to the hospital about how, "that police car pulled right out in front of me."

It is a good thing that I was strapped to that board. I was mad enough to have strangled him. I know we are supposed to forgive and love like Jesus has loved us. That would have to come later. At the moment, I really wanted to hurt him.

When we got to the hospital, I received a CAT scan because of my head injury and an MRI for the neck, back, and knee injuries. My Lieutenant drove over to my house and told my wife what had happened. That had to be traumatic for her but she handled it like a champ. She brought our one year old daughter, Sarah, up to the emergency room. As it turned out, my neck and back injuries were the most serious. Fortunately, I did not require surgery but my back never fully recovered from that accident. After a few hours, I was released from the hospital and my wife drove me home.

Bob, the truck driver, who was in the wrong place at the wrong time, had no serious injuries. He received several cuts from flying glass at the time of impact. The doctors did have to remove some glass from his face and he received a few stitches to close the cuts up.

Timothy, the driver who caused the accident, also did not have any major injuries. It was discovered that he did have cocaine in his system at the time of the accident. He also had a suspended driver's license and no insurance on his car. A number of witnesses told the investigating officers that they had seen Timothy cutting in and out of traffic as he sped up I-85 that morning. He had also been observed using the emergency lane to pass slower traffic.

As he approached the area where I was on the traffic stop, he again tried to use the emergency lane to pass some slower traffic. Only this time, a police car and a large truck happened to be sitting there. He smashed into my police car at about sixty miles an hour. The impact was on the left rear of the police Crown Victoria. The impact knocked me from the driver's seat into the passenger side of the windshield. That is why my head hurt and I had a lump on it. My head hit and cracked the windshield on the passenger side of my patrol car.

At that time, all of our cruisers had a police radio in the center of the front floorboard. When I got hit and knocked into the passenger seat, my right knee smashed into the radio and destroyed it. Fortunately, this was not a serious injury and my knee healed without any lingering after effects.

The officers that investigated the accident charged Timothy with Driving Under the Influence of Drugs, Suspended Driver's License, Reckless Driving, No Insurance and several other traffic charges. The

Accident on the Interstate 41

irony of the situation was that Timothy was driving recklessly that morning because he was running late for his appointment with his probation officer. He was on probation for a previous Driving Under the Influence and drug possession arrest. He ended up getting his probation revoked for these new charges and spending about six months in jail.

A couple of months after this collision, my back injury flared up and I spent almost two weeks in traction at the hospital. My level of injury qualified me for the departmental Purple Heart award. That is not really an award that any officer wants to get.

I was very fortunate to have survived this accident. Other officers have not been so fortunate. A few years after it happened, we had an officer killed in a similar type of incident. Officer Chris McGill, a friend of mine, was part of our DUI Task Force. At the time, those officers were equipped with Ford Mustangs. Another Task Force officer had an impaired driver stopped a few miles south of where my collision took place. Chris came to wait for a tow truck to arrive and impound the violator's vehicle so the arresting officer could start to the jail with his arrestee. While he was seated in his police Mustang, another drunk driver came along and swerved onto the shoulder and smashed into Chris' car. Chris died from his injuries shortly thereafter.

There is no question that being in a smaller car played a significant role in Chris' death. After this happened, our department discontinued the use of the Mustangs for uniformed police work. Thankfully, I was in a full size Ford Crown Victoria when I got hit. There is also no question in my mind that God protected me that morning in 1987.

As a side note to this story, I was out of work for a few days after the initial accident. After the doctor released me to go back to full duty, the first thing that I did was to get back out on I-85 and make a few pullovers. This had been such a close brush with death that I felt fear in the pit of my stomach at the idea of doing any traffic enforcement on the interstate. What if I got hit again? I might not be so lucky next time. I forced myself to make a few traffic stops and write a few tickets. By confronting this fear head-on, it was defeated and I was able to police for another twenty four years without being controlled by fear.

8

I See Dead People

OVER THE YEARS, I have been called to quite a few murder scenes. I described my first homicide in *Street Cop*. In that case, one brother killed the other with an axe. In fact, most murders are domestic related. A husband kills a wife or the wife kills the husband. Brother murders his brother or a son kills his father. Every now and then you come across the homicide that is not domestic related. Many of these are drug related. One doper tries to rip off another doper and somebody ends up getting shot to death. Or a gang member kills a rival gang member as part of an initiation. While that particular killing might not be thought of as a homicide in the truest sense of the word, that is still how it is classified. And then there is the very rare murder in which a completely innocent person is killed. It might be a robbery in which the perp kills the victim so that they can't identify them. We have had cases where a victim just happened to walk into their home as it was being burglarized and ended up getting killed.

While this might sound like a morbid and grotesque chapter, let's be honest. We are all fascinated by serious crime, including murder. Most of the highly watched and highly rated CSI shows involve a homicide in just about every episode. How many movies involve serial killers and the crack Homicide Detectives that track them down? The difference is that the stories I am going to share are real. This chapter will take you inside the crime-scene tape to some of the murders and attempted murders that I have responded to.

In the late eighties and early nineties, crack cocaine had made its appearance and was the drug of choice for many. I was working the night shift in Buford during that time and we saw some violence related to the drug trade. About five in the morning on this particular shift, Sergeant

Dwayne called me on the police radio. He said a citizen had flagged him down and told him that there was a man lying on the side of the interstate in our district. The Sergeant said that he was going to look for him and asked me to come as well. Within just a couple of minutes, Sergeant Dwayne said he was out with an apparent shooting/homicide victim. I joined him a few minutes later.

Sergeant Dwayne and I were out with a dead black male who looked like he was in his twenties. He was lying on his back in the grass next to the interstate. He was obviously dead and had several bullet holes in him. As a uniformed officer, my job when responding to this type of call involves several things. First of all, we have to provide medical care for the injured. In this case, the guy was beyond help. It looked like he had been dead for several hours.

The next thing that uniformed officers need to do is to secure and separate any witnesses. In this case, the only witness that we had was the guy who had notified Sergeant Dwayne. The man had been on his way to work and was already gone. Sergeant Dwayne had alertly obtained his contact information so that the detectives could talk to him later.

The third thing that uniformed officers must do on a call like this is to secure the crime scene. It is vitally important that the scene not be disturbed any more than providing medical treatment and making the scene safe. If the victim is clearly dead, the scene should just be roped off so that no one can enter. This will keep important evidence from being disturbed. I know in the movies, the first officer there will go digging through the victim's pockets, handle a gun that might be laying there, or pick up shell casings or other evidence. In the real world, however, the first officers on the scene should disturb as little as possible. They will rope off the area with crime scene tape and keep a crime scene log of who goes inside the tape.

Sergeant Dwayne called for Homicide Detectives and the CSI Unit to come to the scene. When CSI got there, the first thing that they did was photograph the area. They took a lot of pictures of the victim and the area around him. After the pictures, CSI and the Homicide Detectives did a canvas of the surrounding area. It was pretty clear to all of us that the victim had been driven to the location, taken out of a car and shot to death on the side of the road. Nothing was taken for granted, however. They checked the surrounding area for about a hundred yards in both directions on the possibility that there might be some type of evidence that the perps might have left behind.

After the photographs and a check of the surrounding area, it was time to examine the body before the Medical Examiner took custody of it. The guy was wearing blue jeans and a black t-shirt. He had on socks but no shoes. His jean pockets were turned inside out. There were three one dollar bills lying in the grass next to him. The victim had been shot twice in the chest. He also had a gunshot to the right forearm. It looked like he might have raised his arm to protect himself and took a bullet to the arm. When the detectives rolled him over, we saw another gunshot wound. This one was behind his right ear. Whoever had shot this guy had really wanted him dead.

The detectives had CSI take photographs of all the wounds. They then checked the victim for some identification. He did not have any ID on him. They did find, however, several small baggies of crack cocaine hidden in one of his pockets. That told us that this was not an "innocent" victim. Sure, he probably did not deserve to be executed on the side of the road, but he appeared to have been involved in criminal activity.

I wrote the initial incident report and the Homicide Detectives listed him as a "John Doe" in the morgue. A few days later, a Homicide Detective from the City of Atlanta called. He had gotten wind of the dead guy we had found on the side of the road. After hearing about our case, he drove out and met with our Homicide Detectives working the case. The Atlanta detective had several witnesses who had seen our "victim" selling crack on an Atlanta street corner. The witnesses said that a car had pulled up and three black guys had gotten out, grabbed the drug dealer/victim and shoved him into the car. They then sped off into the night. That was at eleven o'clock the night before we found him shot to death on the interstate thirty miles north of Atlanta.

The Atlanta detective said that there was a major turf war taking place in the city by the various drug gangs. This was not the first guy to be killed. There would probably be a retaliation killing by our victim's gang. That was one of the differences about policing in the suburbs, as opposed to the big city. Our suburban drug dealers seldom resorted to this level of violence. They seemed to feel that there were enough crack addicts to go around. Violence was bad for business!

Probably the most high profile homicide that I was ever involved with took place on May 7, 1993 and it shook the community. I was working the third shift out of our South Precinct. It was late in the shift and I was having trouble keeping my eyes open. The call came out from dispatch as a Person Stabbed call. Officer Ed got the call and I cleared as one of the two backup units. The caller told the dispatcher that he had stabbed his parents and he thought that he had killed his father. I was wide awake now.

Officer Ed got to the scene a couple of minutes before Officer Bruce and I arrived. The neighborhood was a very nice, upper middle class area. Because of the serious nature of the call, I had expected Officer Ed to wait on his backup before going up to the house. One of the common traits that Street Cops have, however, is a desire to be in the middle of the action. Ed was a Street Cop and had already gone up to the house by himself.

When Officer Bruce and I got to the address, we parked and walked cautiously up to the house. The garage door was up and I could see the door leading into the house was standing open. Officer Ed came out leading a handcuffed, young, white guy. The guy looked like he was in his early twenties. He was only wearing a pair of white shorts and he was covered in blood. He looked like he had the starring role in a slasher movie. There was blood on his chest, arms, hands, legs and shorts.

Officer Ed said, "When I got here, he met me in the garage and told me that he had killed his father and maybe his mother. I'm going to get him secured in my police car and call the Sergeant and the Homicide Detectives if you guys want to clear the house."

Bruce and I pulled our pistols out and started clearing the house. Our intent was to start on the ground level and work our way through the large house. There is a real science to how to safely clear a building. Officers typically will take their time, safely clearing one room at a time. When we got in the house, however, we knew that we were going to have to speed the process up.

"Help me! Please help me!" The weak female voice was coming from upstairs. The voice sounded muffled, like the person was in a closet.

Bruce and I visually cleared what we could as we worked our way towards the stairs. The voice continued to call, "Please hurry. My husband is hurt. I am hurt. Please help me!"

Even though we wanted to help the person behind the voice, we also did not want to rush headlong into another perp. The guy that Ed had was probably the only bad guy but we did not know that for sure.

When we got to the top of the stairs, we saw an open bedroom door. There was a blood trail from that bedroom into the hallway. The voice was coming from inside that bedroom. "Oh God! Will someone please help us? My husband is hurt. We need help!"

As Bruce and I stepped into the bedroom, it looked like a scene from a slasher movie. The carpet was covered with blood. The white bed sheets were splattered with blood. In the middle of the floor, a large man lay on his back. He was only wearing white Fruit of the Loom briefs that were stained red. He was a big man, probably six foot four and around two hundred and sixty pounds. The big man was obviously dead. He had multiple stab wounds to his chest, abdomen, neck, and throat. There was a medium size butcher knife lying on the floor a few feet away from him.

The voice was coming from the bathroom that was connected to the bedroom. The bathroom door was closed, but bore the marks of the axe that was lying next it. The door had been smashed and had several holes in it. Officer Bruce told the voice that it was the police and we were there to help.

The bathroom door opened and a woman came out. She was covered in blood. She had stab wounds in the neck, throat, face, back, arms, and hands. She had a towel around her neck and a towel around her hand. I had just heard over the police radio that the ambulance had arrived. Officer Bruce went down to bring the paramedics upstairs.

The woman was in shock. When she came out of the bathroom, she saw her husband lying in the floor. "Is he okay?" she asked.

"The paramedics are coming up now," I told her. "They are going to check you and your husband."

I guided the woman out in the hallway to get her out of the room with her dead husband. Since the woman was walking, the paramedics quickly led her down the stairs and started working on her. She had been stabbed sixteen times. The paramedics quickly prepared her to be transported and got her onto the stretcher.

"What about my husband?" the woman asked a paramedic.

"We are still working on him, ma'am," she was told.

A couple of the firemen that were also paramedics did go and check on the man. They confirmed that he was dead. The woman was transported to the hospital. We found out that her name was Judy. Judy required extensive surgeries. The most serious was to repair her vocal chords. She had been stabbed in the throat and after the adrenaline wore off, she could only speak in a whisper. One of her thumbs had almost been severed from her hand, and she also required quite a bit of plastic surgery where she had been stabbed in the face.

Judy's husband, Chuck, was a much loved high school football coach at Parkview High School in Lilburn. His murder and the attempted murder of Judy shocked the community. What made it even more shocking was that their son, Chip, was the perpetrator. This was a bizarre story. Chip was well known in the community, too. He was a karate instructor at a local martial arts school and was loved by his students.

Chip had a dark side, though, that became known after he was arrested and charged with the murder of his father and the attempted murder of his mother. He had been living a lie for the last six years. Chip was a poor student and had failed out in his first semester at college. He knew that his parents really wanted him to go to college so for the next several years, he pretended to go to school every day. His parents even took him out to dinner to celebrate his graduation. The problem was there had been no graduation. It was all a lie.

When his parents asked to see his diploma, he stalled them, saying that he was getting it framed. After a couple of weeks, however, Chip's parents suspected something was up. Another argument on May 6, 1993, led to their demand to see Chip's non-existent college diploma the next day.

It was late that night that Chip crept into his parent's bedroom with a flashlight and a knife. He stabbed his mother first, getting her in the neck. His father, Chuck, was awake immediately and came to his wife's defense. Chip quickly turned the knife on his father. Chuck yelled at his son, "Wake up, Chip, you're having a nightmare!" Chip was wide awake and continued to struggle with his father, stabbing him repeatedly.

Judy heard the struggle and saw the shadows as the two men fought in the dark. She heard Chip making karate yells. Chuck cried out, "Oh my God, Chip, you don't know what you're doing! Call 911." Those were his last words as the big man fell to the floor.

Judy knew that she was next. She ran into the bathroom. The door did not have a lock so she put her feet against the toilet and her back against the door to try and keep it closed. Judy grabbed a towel and wrapped it around her bleeding neck. Chip tried to pry the door open and then started kicking it. When that didn't work, he yelled, "You're ruining my plan!"

He left for a few minutes but returned with an axe. The blade barely missed Judy's head as it smashed through the bathroom door. She knew that she could not stay where she was. She flung open the bathroom door and yelled, "You're not going to kill me with an axe!"

Chip charged her as she ran out of the bathroom. He dropped the axe and picked his knife back up, stabbing his mother repeatedly as he chased her around the bedroom and out into the hallway. Judy kept yelling at him to stop and call 911 for his father. Finally, something seemed to register with Chip. Judy said, "He sort of came to. He dropped the knife and went right over to the phone and called 911. When the police came, he let them in."

The District Attorney was originally going to seek the Death Penalty against Chip. In the end, however, Judy agreed to a Life Sentence plus five years for her son to avoid the turmoil of a long and painful trial. Chip entered his Guilty Plea on February 21, 1994 and is still serving his sentence in a Georgia prison.[1]

Believe it or not, some of the most serious calls even have a comic side to them. I responded to an attempted murder that came in as a Home Invasion Call. The female caller said that her husband had been shot. The dispatcher said that the lady sounded intoxicated and the only description of a suspect was a black male. The dispatcher also said that she could hear a male screaming in the background, "Help me!"

Officer Doug and I got to the apartment complex at the same time. The apartment numbers indicated that it was on the upper landing. Doug and I quietly worked our way up the stairs. We did not know if the perp was still around. We approached the door of the apartment and listened at the door. We could hear voices inside. A pained male voice said, "Why did you do that?"

I knocked on the door and announced, "Police Department!"

Doug and I had our pistols out. The door opened and a very drunk white female, Stephanie, motioned for us to come in. We were not going to rush into a possible ambush, so we asked her to step out of the apartment. Stephanie stepped out into the landing and said, "My husband needs an ambulance. He has been shot."

"Who shot him? Where are they now?" I asked.

1. http://www.bullshido.net/forums/showthread.php?t=3242&page=1.

Stephanie said slowly, "It was a black guy. He broke into our apartment and shot Joe. Then he left."

Doug and I looked at the front door and then at each other. There was no damage to the door or any indication that someone had forced their way in through that door. "Did the guy break in through the front door?" I asked.

"Yep," Stephanie replied, nodding her head.

We needed to check on Joe and see how badly he was hurt. I could hear the siren of the ambulance as it entered the apartment complex. "You don't have any weapons on you, do you?" I asked Stephanie.

"No, you can check me," she said. Doug did a quick pat down to confirm that she was unarmed. Her story was not adding up. We entered the apartment. Joe was lying in a pool of blood on the kitchen floor. It looked like he had been shot in the leg. He was holding a towel to the wound and looked like he was in a lot of pain. Leg wounds can be very dangerous and many people have bled to death after having their femoral artery severed. Joe was leaking a lot of blood.

There was a small .38 Special revolver laying the kitchen counter. "Whose gun?" Doug asked, slipping it into his back pocket to secure it.

As I said before, when there is a crime scene, officers should not disturb any more than what is absolutely necessary. In this case, Officer Doug understood that our safety took precedent over anything else. There was no way that he was going to leave a loaded pistol laying out where anyone could grab it.

"The black guy must have dropped it there," Stephanie said.

I looked at Joe. "The ambulance will be here in just a minute. Keep that pressure on the wound," I told him. "Tell me what happened."

Joe looked at me and then looked at Stephanie. Joe was pretty drunk himself, as it turned out.

Stephanie spoke for him. "Honey, I told them about the black guy that broke in and shot you."

"Yeah," said Joe. "This black guy broke in and shot me."

I asked Officer Doug to take Stephanie into another room. When they had left the kitchen, I spoke to Joe again. "Look, Joe. It's obvious that that is not what happened. What were you guys arguing about and why did Stephanie shoot you?"

Joe's eyes got big and he said, "How did you know? Okay, I'll tell you what happened. But I want you to understand, I am not pressing charges."

"No problem. Tell me about it."

You know it is going to be a good story when it starts out with, "Well, we were at the bar up the street drinking . . ."

He continued, "We were there for a while and we both had a good bit to drink. Stephanie thought that I was talking to this other girl at the bar and she kind of got pissed. She made a big scene at the bar so we left. When we got home, she just could not let it go and kept yelling at me about talking to another woman. I finally had had enough and I told her that I was leaving. That was when she grabbed the gun. She told me that I was not going anywhere and she shot me."

"So, then what happened?"

"Well, after she shot me, she realized what she had done and started telling me how sorry she was. She called 911 and I heard her tell them that a black guy had broken in and shot me."

By now, the paramedics were in the apartment and were working on Joe. Thankfully for him, Stephanie had not hit the big artery that goes through the leg. If she had, he would have probably bled to death already. Leg wounds can be very serious.

Officer Doug and Stephanie came back into the kitchen as the paramedics were getting ready to wheel Joe out to the ambulance on a stretcher. I told Stephanie that she was under arrest for Attempted Murder and handcuffed her. Joe saw what was going on and said, "Wait a minute! I said that I was not going to press charges."

"I know what you said, Joe," I told him. "This falls under the Domestic Violence Law and I am going to be the one who presses charges."

I don't know whatever happened with Joe and Stephanie. I know that when the case went to trial, Joe refused to testify against her. In the end, she pleaded guilty to Aggravated Assault. Because of the circumstances, however, she did not get any prison time, just probation and a fine. And probably an Anger Management Course!

9

A Midnight Swim

SERGEANT CARLOS AND I responded to an aggravated domestic call one warm summer's night. It was about one in the morning. The dispatcher told us that the male caller had stated that a former girlfriend was stalking him. When she gave the address, I recognized the home as one that we had been to several times recently. It was located on several acres of land in a rural area of the county near Buford. He had reported previously that his ex was coming out there in the middle of the night and vandalizing his house, and that she had slashed all four of the tires on his pickup truck. The girl, Susan, had been arrested on these charges several months before and had just gotten out of jail. She was being much more careful this time and was always gone by the time the police arrived. We had taken several reports for him and there were already new warrants out for Susan. We had even been checking his property a few times a night but had been unable to catch the girl in action.

When I arrived at the house, I spoke to the resident. He was a middle aged white guy named Frank. Frank was balding and a bit overweight. He told me, "Susan just left. She was pounding on my door saying she wanted to talk to me. She said she forgave me for having her arrested and was willing to take me back."

Frank said he did not even go to the door. He just called the police. He said, "You guys got here pretty quick. She may still be hiding on the property somewhere."

About that time, Sergeant Carlos was pulling down the driveway, so I told Frank we would take a walk around his property. He lived on several acres and was about five hundred feet off of the road. I asked

Frank, "I'm not trying to be nosy, but we are out here all the time on this girl. How in the world did you hook up with her in the first place?"

Frank said, "Officer, I met her through one of those classified ads in the newspaper. We went out one time for dinner. Dinner led to a few drinks and we came back here and spent the night together. The next day, she asked if she could move in. When I told her, 'No,' she went crazy and started screaming that she was going to kill me. She trashed the inside of my house before I could get her to leave. After that, she started calling everyday and either threatening to kill me or offering to come over and make up. Then she started vandalizing my stuff, slashing my tires, and breaking in when I wasn't here. I thought that having her arrested would stop it but as soon as she got out of jail, she was back."

This sounded like a Hollywood screenplay. I related to Sergeant Carlos what I knew and we pulled out our flashlights and started walking and looking at potential hiding places around the house. *There is no way she is still here*, I thought. *She knows she is going back to jail if we catch her.*

The area around the house was clear and we started walking through the big yard. It was a nice night. There was a full moon shining and it was not too humid. There was a clump of trees off to the side of the house about a hundred feet away. We decided we would check the trees and then call it off. When we were about fifty feet away from the trees, we were startled by a figure jumping up from behind a tree and running deeper into the woods.

As we chased the figure into the woods, we were trying to not run into a tree, not trip over a root, and not get ambushed and shot. We could hear the person that we were chasing ahead of us crashing through the woods. It did not look like they had a flashlight. Sergeant Carlos and I ran for a couple of hundred yards and then stopped to listen. The woods were quiet except for our heavy breathing. Then, just ahead of us, we heard a splash and a woman screaming.

Another fifty yards ahead of us, we found a small pond. It was about an acre in size. We found out later, we had run over to Frank's next door neighbor's property. This was his pond. In the middle of the pond we could see a female, Susan, thrashing around. She looked like she was trying to swim to the other side of the pond, still a considerable distance away. Sergeant Carlos yelled, "Susan, come on out of there! You can't get away."

Susan yelled back, "I'm not going back to jail! Why can't you just leave me and Frank alone? He loves me."

By this time, Susan was over fifty feet out in the pond. I shined my light in the water. It was black and murky and had green scum on the surface. I involuntarily shuddered, thinking about what might be swimming beneath the surface. After a few more minutes of splashing, Susan ran out of gas and began to scream, "I can't swim anymore! Help me!"

I could see her head going under and then coming back up as she gasped and sputtered. I caught movement out of the corner of my eye and saw that Sergeant Carlos had taken his gun belt off. He sat on the ground and was taking his boots and socks off. "Sarge, what are you doing?" I asked. "You aren't planning on going in the water are you?"

"We can't let her drown," he said. Now he was taking his shirt off.

Susan continued to scream. "Please help me! I can't swim! I can't float!" She went under again and came up coughing.

"Sarge, we didn't put her in that pond. She chose to get in there to try and get away from us. Let's call the Fire Department. They can bring their boat out here to try and get her."

"That will take too long. She will already have drowned and I don't want that on my conscience," Sergeant Carlos said. He was taking his bullet proof vest off.

I tried another approach. "Sarge, I am not a very good swimmer. If you get out there and get in trouble, I am not going to be able to help you. You are going to be on your own."

Carlos was on his feet and starting for the water. "I am a trained lifeguard and a very strong swimmer," he said. "I'll be OK."

As he was just about to enter the murky pond, I tried one more time to keep my Sergeant out of the water. "Sarge, you know there are probably water moccasins in there. That pond has got be full of snakes. Look at that nasty water."

That got his attention. He turned around and looked at me and said, "I never thought about snakes. I hate snakes. Let's call the Fire Department."

Susan continued to scream and it looked like she was probably going to drown. I can't say that I felt sorry for her. She was clearly crazy, was making Frank's life a living hell, and had now put herself in a really bad position. Nope, this was not my problem. I called the dispatcher and requested the Fire Department's Water Rescue Unit to be enroute. They would be there in about thirty minutes, the dispatcher told me a couple of minutes later.

In the meantime, Sergeant Carlos had put his socks and boots back on. He then started walking around the edge of the pond, obviously looking for something. Susan's screams were starting to become periodic moans as she went under and then came up coughing. Carlos found what he was looking for about a quarter of the way around the pond. I saw him get into a metal canoe and push out into the pond.

In just a few minutes he had paddled out to where Susan was. He grabbed her by collar and told her to hold onto the side of the boat while he paddled to the shore. The crazy woman almost tipped the canoe over but he managed to steer the boat to where I was waiting. When he was only a few feet from the shore, Susan tried to break away back out into the middle of the pond. The Sergeant used the wooden oar that he was holding and shoved her towards me. I grabbed her and drug her out of the water onto the dry ground. She quickly got to her feet and became combative. I slammed her down hard on the ground, knocking the breath and some nasty pond water out of her. We got her handcuffed and searched.

I called radio and told them to cancel the Fire Department. Then the Sergeant and I realized that we had our work cut out for us. We were several hundred yards from our cars in a thick patch of woods. We were going to have to escort Crazy Susan out of the woods and she wasn't really in a cooperative mood. The other problem was that she really smelled bad. Marinating in that smelly pond water had given her a unique odor. The idea of putting her in my police car and having to drive her to the jail twenty minutes away needed to be reconsidered.

"Hey, Sarge. What do you think about having the Rookie come over here and handle this? This would be a good case for him."

The "Rookie" was Officer Gilbert. He was brand new and had only been on his own for a few weeks. "That is an excellent idea," said Sergeant Carlos. He called Gilbert on the radio and told him to join us.

We found a shortcut out of the woods and were making our way towards our police cars. By now, all of the fight had left Susan and she was just a smelly, crazy woman. "Can I see Frank before you take me away? I want to tell him how much I love him. He loves me too. I can tell."

Officer Gilbert got there and we put the nasty woman in his car. I told him that I would do the report if he would just transport Susan to the jail and take out the Stalking warrant on her. With this new criminal charge, the existing ones, and a Probation Violation charge, she would be in jail for about a year. We never got any more calls to Frank's house so I guess Susan finally got the hint that it was over between her and Frank. Officer Gilbert did tell me, though, that it was weeks before he got that nasty smell out of his car.

10

Violent Crack Head

This incident took place in 1991, not long after the Los Angeles Police Department had become infamous for their beating of a violent crack head named Rodney King. I was working the overnight shift in the Buford area. The call came in as Vandalism in Progress and was in the black section of town. The dispatcher told me that this was also an Aggravated Domestic call. The guy who was doing the vandalism was the brother of the caller.

My backup unit on the call was Officer Ted. He was the only other officer that was not out on another call. He told me where he was coming from and I knew that I was going to be on my own for a few minutes. I was nearby when the call was dispatched and was probably there in less than five minutes.

I pulled up and stopped one house down from the address I was going to. It is not a good idea to stop right in front of the house that you are dispatched to. That is a good way to get shot. I left my parking lights on, turned the police car off and pocketed the keys. Leaving the parking lights on was a trick that a veteran officer had taught me early on. By doing so, it was much easier for other officers to find you at night when you needed help. It was also never a good idea to leave the keys in the ignition. Suspects have been known to steal police cars. It is always embarrassing when you have to call your Sergeant and tell him that your police car had been stolen.

All of the houses in this area are old and small. I walked up to the small, white, square house and knocked on the door. I could see that two of the front windows were broken. I could not hear anything through the thin walls of the house. Everything was quiet. The front door opened and a young black lady, LaTasha, identified herself as the caller. It was obvious that she had been crying.

LaTasha told me that her brother was back on crack cocaine. She and her husband had taken him in to try and help him. Tonight, though, he came home after smoking crack and wanted to fight with LaTasha and her husband, Scott. At that moment, Scott came walking up to where we were standing inside the front door. He was a really big guy and it was clear that he was angry.

Scott said, "I didn't want to take him in but he is my wife's brother. We have two small kids and they don't need to see some crazy crack head acting the fool. LaTasha wanted to help him but now I want him gone!"

LaTasha started crying again. I asked her what her brother's name was. She said, "His name is Reginald but we call him Reggie. He is really a nice guy when he is not on crack."

"Well, he is back on crack and I don't want him around our kids," Scott said.

I asked them about the vandalism that they had reported. Scott said, "When Reggie started yelling and cussing at LaTasha, and acting a fool, I grabbed him and threw him out the front door. I didn't hit him or anything, Officer. I just threw him outside and locked the door."

"After Scott threw him out, that's when Reggie broke the windows. I think he hit them with a stick or something," LaTasha said.

"Do you have any idea where Reggie might have gone?" I asked.

"He don't have anywhere else to go," said LaTasha. "We are his only family."

At that comment, Scott rolled his eyes. I got the information that I needed to make a report of the incident. They gave me a physical description and told me what he was wearing. I told Scott and LaTasha to call us if Reggie showed back up. I also told them that before I left, I would walk around the house and make sure that Reggie wasn't still lurking around. I figured he was gone to wherever angry crack heads go to hide from the police or an angry brother-in-law.

My backup, Officer Ted, still had not arrived but I did not give it much thought. Reggie was long gone, or so I thought. I walked around the side of Scott and LaTasha's house. I was cautious as I walked around the residence. You never rush around corners because someone might be waiting on you. Someone like Reggie.

As I quick peeked around the corner into the backyard, my flashlight picked up a figure about twenty feet away, walking quickly in the opposite direction. I challenged him, "Reggie, it's the Police. Stop right there!"

Reggie stopped and turned around. The backyard was dark. The only light came from my flashlight. I could see that he was breathing hard and was clenching and unclenching his fists. His eyes were glazed over but had a wild look in them. "Reggie, we need to talk. Can you come over here?"

Reggie did not move but said, "I don't need to talk to you. I ain't done nothing and I ain't going back to jail."

Now I wondered, *Where is Ted at?* I called him over the radio and asked him for an ETA. He said he would be there in a minute or two. I just needed to stall for time.

"Jail? Who said anything about jail? I just wanted to get your side of what happened tonight."

Reggie wasn't convinced. "You cops never listen to me. I'm not going to jail. I'll mess you up if you try to take me."

I could see him continuing to clench and unclench his fists. This was about to get interesting. While Reggie was talking, I had taken a couple of steps towards him. *Come on, Ted. Hurry up*, I thought. Reggie was about five feet nine inches tall and skinny. He did not look very imposing but crack cocaine could make a Chihuahua think it was a German Shepherd. I was six foot two and about two hundred and twenty pounds. I have been involved in some type of martial arts for most of my life. At that time, I was training several evenings a week in Wing Chun Kung Fu. I received my first black belt the year before. Guys like Reggie gave me a real life training opportunity. What other job gave you this kind of fun?

Reggie saw me step forward and he took the bait. He started towards me. *Thanks, Reggie!*

He said, "I told you I'll mess you up."

He covered the distance in just a second. He was ready to fight. I was glad that I had put my leather gloves on as I had gotten out of my police car. As soon as he was in range, Reggie started punching. He was flailing wildly trying to hit me in the face. I took a quick step back and to the side, allowing the first barrage of punches to miss. As Reggie surged forward again to try and hit me, I stepped in with a straight punch that landed flush on his nose. The impact was doubled because he was coming forward when I hit him. I felt his nose go flat with the punch's impact. Reggie's head snapped back and his knees buckled. I swept his feet out from under him and dropped him on his face. I planted my two hundred and twenty pounds onto Reggie's back and heard the breath driven out of him.

Now, I had to get Reggie handcuffed. His hands were underneath him and he was still combative. When he got his wind back, Reggie started screaming, "Help! The police are beating me! Help!"

This would have been humorous except for the fact that Rodney King was still fresh on people's minds and I was in a black neighborhood. *Where was Officer Ted?* I called him on the radio and told him I needed some help. He said he was having trouble finding me. He asked for a description of the house.

I told him, "It is the one with the police car parked next to it!"

The back door opened and the back porch light came on. Reggie continued to scream that I was beating him. LaTasha came out and saw me on top of Reggie and said, "What are you doing to him?"

I said, "Ma'am, I'm not hurting him. He was trying to fight me and I am just holding him down until the other officer gets here. When he gets here we can get Reggie handcuffed and get him some help."

This was basically true. She could not see his broken nose because his face was pressed into the ground and I was not beating him. One punch had done the trick. Whenever Officer Ted got there, we could get him handcuffed without having to hurt him anymore. And we would get Reggie some help. Although by help, I meant taking him to jail where he could not purchase any crack cocaine for a long time.

Reggie continued to scream while I waited for Ted. I saw Scott come to the back door and look out. He saw me on top of Reggie, nodded approvingly, and went back into the house. The neighbors on either side of LaTasha and Scott came out in their backyards in response to Reggie's screams. I was easily holding him down, but he was screaming like a girl.

I heard one of the neighbors say, "Oh, it looks like the police are beating another black man!" *Hurry up, Ted!*

LaTasha came to my defense and said, "He's not beating him. He is just holding him down until another officer gets here. They are going to try and get him some help. Reggie was acting crazy and trying to fight everybody."

This quieted the neighbor. *God bless you, LaTasha!* I heard tires squealing down the street and in just a moment, Officer Ted came running around the side of the house. Reggie was still resisting but he was starting to wind down. We got him handcuffed without too much trouble. When we stood him up, I kept his back to LaTasha so she could not see his face. I had not done anything wrong but the sight of her brother's blood might have been upsetting. His nose was flattened and there was a lot of blood on his face and the front of his shirt. We walked him around to the front yard and over to my police car and got him secured.

Officer Ted stood guard and I went and spoke to LaTasha. I told her about my encounter with Reggie. I let her know that I had only hit him once and his nose was bleeding a little. She was very understanding.

She said, "I know he was acting crazy. Thank you for not beating him. Maybe he can get some help."

When I got back to my police car, Officer Ted was very apologetic. He did not try to make excuses. He said, "I got lost. I get turned around on these city streets. I am sorry I made you wait."

I told him not to worry about it. Everything worked out okay. Ted turned out to be a really good officer. Now I just had to get Reggie to the jail. I was a little concerned that the jail would not accept him. They might want me to take him to the hospital first. His nose was a mess but other than cleaning it there wasn't much they could do for it. I really did not want to have to sit at the hospital for two or three hours with Reggie while I waited on them to treat him. I figured I would try the jail first. They had a nurse there that could check him.

The closer we got to the jail, the more agitated Reggie got. He kept telling me that as soon as they took his handcuffs off, he was really going to mess me up. I laughed at him and asked, "How is your nose feeling, Reggie? It doesn't look too good." Reggie told me to do something physically impossible.

When we arrived at the jail, I called the deputies over the radio and told them I had a combative prisoner. There is nothing that makes their night like when the police bring in someone that wants to fight. Several deputies were waiting for me when I pulled in. They were all big men and looking expectant. One of them opened my back door and saw Reggie's mangled nose.

The deputy said, "Hey, this guy may need to go to the hospital and get checked out."

As the words were leaving the deputy's mouth, Reggie let go with a stream of bloody spit that landed on the deputy's leg. *Thanks Reggie!* The deputy roared, "You son of a bitch!"

The group of deputies moved in mass and snatched Reggie out of my car and dropped him on the pavement in the parking area. They roughly dragged/carried him into the jail and deposited him in a holding cell. There was no more talk of me needing to take him to the hospital.

I charged Reggie with Vandalism, because of the damage he had done to Scott and LaTasha's house. I charged him with Simple Assault and Felony Resisting Arrest for my little tussle with him. Since Reggie was already on probation, he spent close to a year in custody.

11

Tough Guy

Corporal Chuck and I pulled into the rundown apartment complex in the little town of Sugar Hill. The call had come from a woman who wanted to turn her boyfriend in. She had told the dispatcher that he was wanted on an outstanding Probation Violation warrant and was currently passed out on her couch. Chuck and I had already confirmed with our dispatcher that the warrant was still active. Ricky was wanted for Probation Violation but the original charges were several counts of Burglary. He had broken into a number of people's homes in the Buford/Sugar Hill area. He also had an extensive criminal history for Motor Vehicle Theft, Assault, Drugs, and Resisting Arrest. This might be a fun call.

Rhonda met us in front of her apartment. As she puffed on her cigarette, she told us that she was tired of Ricky's drunken tirades. "He's fine when he's sober," she said, "but he ain't sober much. He hasn't given me any rent money for three months and I'm about to lose my apartment."

Chuck asked Rhonda where Ricky was in the apartment. She told us that he was on the couch just inside the front door. She went on to say, "Now, I just want to let you know, Ricky likes to fight. It took four or five officers the last time the police came to get him."

Chuck and I were the only two officers available. Everyone else was handling other calls. Chuck and I had worked together enough that we felt comfortable going in and getting Ricky. Chuck is a big guy. He is about six foot one and weighs about two hundred and fifty pounds. He was a regular in the gym and was very strong. I am six foot two and weighed about two hundred and twenty pounds at the time.

We asked Rhonda to wait outside while we went in to arrest Ricky. He was lying on his back on the couch just like Rhonda had told us.

All he had on were his boxer shorts. He woke up immediately when we walked in. His eyes darted from Chuck to me to the front door. Chuck said, "Hey Ricky, you have a warrant out for you so we have to take you in. Do you want to put some pants on?"

Ricky sat up on the couch and rubbed the sleep out of his eyes. "Did Rhonda turn me in?" he asked.

"It really doesn't matter who turned you in," I told him. "The warrant is valid so we don't have any choice. We have to arrest you."

Ricky stood up and slipped on his blue jeans. He had long stringy blond hair. He was about five foot ten and weighed about two hundred pounds. He had a bit of a beer gut, but he was acting like he was resigned to be going back to jail. Then he asked, "Can I talk to my girlfriend first?"

Chuck said, "No, Ricky, we can't let you do that. Are you going to put on a shirt and some shoes?"

Ricky immediately went from compliant to belligerent. "I'm not going anywhere until I talk to my girlfriend. Rhonda? Rhonda, did you turn me in?" he yelled out the open front door.

Chuck and I moved in unison and grabbed Ricky to handcuff him. Ricky wasn't as drunk as Rhonda had made him sound like because he reacted quickly and punched Chuck in the chest, shoved past me, and then bolted through the front door into the parking lot. I was right on his heels and tackled him in the parking lot next to our two police cars. He immediately squirmed away from me and managed to get to his feet. Ricky started throwing punches wildly at both of us.

I ducked back out of the way to avoid getting hit by one of those wild swings. Chuck dove in and tackled Ricky again and slammed him down hard on the asphalt. Ricky kept fighting and squirmed away from Chuck. I punched him several times in the body as he was trying to get to his feet. I also snapped his head back with a hard straight left. Ricky tried to break away again and run as Chuck was trying to get back to his feet. I grabbed Ricky again around the torso and shoved him towards Chuck's police car. He tried to hit me in the groin with his knee. I was able to shift out of the way and took the knee strikes on the leg.

Chuck punched Ricky a couple of times in the face while I was still holding him. I felt the power from those punches. So did Ricky. He started to sag a little bit now. I threw him back down onto the parking lot face first. Chuck and I both got on his back and tried to get him handcuffed. Ricky tried a couple of times to throw us off but two hard punches to the kidneys took the last bit of fight out of him. We finally were able to get him handcuffed.

Chuck and I looked at each other. We were both winded. Chuck's shirt was ripped from where Ricky had grabbed him at some point during the fight. We both had scratches and scrapes on our arms and knees from fighting on the asphalt parking lot. Other than that, we were in pretty good shape.

Ricky, however, did not look too good. His nose was bleeding, his lower lip was busted and bleeding, and one of his eyes was starting to swell noticeably. Since he did not have a shirt on, he also had a number of scrapes and scratches from rolling around on the asphalt. While he was lying there handcuffed, Ricky looked up at Corporal Chuck and me. He told us defiantly, "Okay, you may have whipped my ass, but it took two of you to do it!"

We just laughed at him. As we started to get Ricky to his feet and put him in Chuck's police car, I looked around for Rhonda. She had already gone back into her apartment and shut the door. Chuck told Ricky, "You know, Ricky, you violated one of the first rules of being a successful criminal. You pissed your girlfriend off and so she called the police and turned you in."

Ricky stared at us and actually looked like he was going to cry. "What do you mean?" he asked. "I just gave her my whole paycheck. I only kept out enough money to get some beer. I gave her the rest."

"That's not what she said," I told him as we sat him in the police car. "She says you haven't given her any money in months."

"That's not true! Rhonda! Why did you lie to these officers?" he yelled at the apartment. "You know I just gave you over four hundred dollars!"

By this time, Chuck and I both believed him. He probably had given his money to Rhonda. By turning Ricky in, she knows he will be gone for a while and she can go shopping or buy some drugs. After the fight that Ricky had given us, though, we did not feel very sorry for him.

12

Just Another Afternoon in the Trailer Park

(or a Redneck Paternity Test)

THE CALL TO THE Buford Mobile Home Park came out as an, "Active Fight." The caller said that the two males were punching each other in the face and rolling around on the ground. *Just another Saturday in Buford,* I thought. I was close to the trailer park when I got the call, so I was there within a couple of minutes of being dispatched. It was about five o'clock in the afternoon when I arrived at the single-wide mobile home. It was still daylight and I could see that the yard was empty. I was kind of disappointed. I had been hoping that they would still be fighting when I got there. The front door of the trailer opened and two white guys with beards stepped out. It wasn't hard to tell that they had been the ones fighting. They were both wearing t-shirts and blue jeans. I could see that their t-shirts were ripped and covered with grass stains. They both had grass in their hair. The taller of the two, Robby, had a bloody nose. The other guy, Jimmy, had a busted lip.

They walked slowly over to my police car. I got out and said, "What's going on, guys?"

Neither one answered right away. They shoved their hands in their pockets, hung their heads, and kicked at the ground. They both had guilty looks. They reminded me of children caught doing something wrong by their parent. Jimmy finally spoke up. "We just had a little disagreement, officer. It's kind of embarrassing."

Robby added, "It was all my fault, officer. I said something I shouldn't have said."

The front door of the trailer opened again and a very large woman stepped out. She had to have weighed at least three hundred pounds. She walked over to where we were at. Robby and Jimmy didn't weigh three hundred pounds together. Jimmy motioned at her with his head and said, "That's my wife, Tina"

"So, Tina, what were these guys fighting about?" I asked.

Tina turned a scornful eye at both men, who were both still gazing at the ground. She said, "The main problem is that they are both stupid! Robby is my ex-husband. We are still real good friends. Him and his new wife came over for dinner tonight. Jimmy and me has been married about a year and we just had our first kid. Well, after dinner, I was holding the baby and Robby says, '"I wonder if that is my baby."' He was just kidding but Jimmy didn't think it was funny. One thing led to another and then they was fighting in the front yard."

"Is there any reason why Robby would have said such a thing?" I asked Tina.

Now it was Tina's turn to hang her head. She said, "Well, me and Robby got back together a couple of months after me and Jimmy got married. It was just a fling for a few days and then I realized I really did want to be with Jimmy. I went back to Jimmy and got pregnant right after we got back together."

By now, I felt like I was on the set of The Jerry Springer Show. We just needed one more fat chick and a camera crew. "How did you guys resolve this?" I asked the two men. "Are you going to do a paternity test?"

Robby and Jimmy both looked puzzled. Jimmy asked, "What's that?"

"You know." I answered. "It's a test to determine who the father is."

"Oh, yeah," Jimmy said. "We already did that."

Robby said, "Yeah, we held little Joey up next to both of us and we all decided he has Jimmy's eyes and looks a lot more like him than he does me."

Jimmy broke into a big semi-toothless grin. "He's got my eyes," he repeated.

"Well, that does sound pretty scientific," I acknowledged. "So, you guys are both happy with that and you aren't going to be fighting anymore?"

"Oh, no sir!" came their answer.

"We're glad we were able to work it out," said Jimmy. He and Robby shook hands in my presence to signify that they were friends again.

As I turned to get into my police car, I said, "Tina, you keep them straight, okay?"

"If they start fighting again," she answered, "I'll just grab both of them in a headlock and squeeze until they give up."

I have no doubt that she could have done just that.

13

When You Gotta Go . . .

It was another quiet midnight shift in Buford and there wasn't much going on. When the Aggravated Domestic call came out on the radio, three of us cleared on it. The dispatcher said that the wife had called on her husband because he was yelling at her. The husband had immediately called the police himself and said that his wife was the one doing the yelling. Normally, only two officers would respond to this type of call but I was bored and decided to go with Officer Tim and Officer Leroy.

The home that we were responding to was a double-wide trailer just outside of town. We all got there at about the same time. As we got out of our police cars, we could hear the couple yelling at each other all the way out in the front yard. When Tim knocked on the front door, a young, crying, white woman opened the door. She motioned for us to come in. Her husband, a white guy with long hair and a bushy beard, was sitting on the couch. I did not see any visible injuries on either person. If neither party was injured, then we could probably resolve this without someone getting arrested.

The best way to handle most domestic calls is for the officers to separate the subjects and talk to them on either ends of the house. This serves two purposes. First of all, it gives both of them a chance to calm down. Secondly, it allows the officers to get an uninterrupted version of what had happened. After the officers have interviewed the subjects involved, they will then compare stories and decide what action, if any, needs to be taken.

Officer Tim asked the wife, Lisa, if he could talk to her. They stepped down the short hallway into a bedroom. Officer Leroy stayed in the living room with the husband, TJ. I stood near the front door. I could see into the bedroom where Tim was talking to Lisa and I could see and hear Leroy's interview with TJ. It did not appear that either one of them had been drinking. That was unusual. Very few domestic calls involved two sober people. Usually one, and if we were lucky, both, of them would be drunk.

TJ told Leroy that they were arguing about money. Lisa's parents had helped them to buy their double-wide a few years before. Lisa needed another car and her parents were offering to buy it for her. TJ felt that they were trying to control Lisa and him with their money.

I was listening to TJ and Leroy talk but I was watching Tim, making sure he was okay. He did not seem to be listening to Lisa and kept glancing back up the hallway at me. I then heard him say to her, "Let's go back out here."

They came back into the living room. Tim told Lisa to sit down on the couch next to TJ. I figured he was about to lecture them on behaving like children, or something similar. Instead, he surprised all of us by asking, "Where is your restroom?"

TJ pointed back down the hallway. "First door on the right."

Tim almost sprinted into the restroom. We could hear the "snap," as he undid his belt keepers. There was a loud thump as his gun belt hit the floor. Leroy and I just stood there in the living room with TJ and Lisa. No one said anything. It was a bit awkward. I had never been on a call where an officer had had to relieve himself in the middle of a family fight. Leroy told TJ and Lisa, "Sorry about this. He has some stomach issues."

The couple just nodded at him. After a few minutes, we heard the toilet flush. Tim came out of the bathroom putting on his belt keepers. He walked back into the living room and asked the now silent couple, "Do y'all need us anymore?"

Whatever they had been arguing over was long forgotten. The police officer who had to take a crap during their domestic dispute seemed to have diffused their anger. We let ourselves out into the darkness. When we got back to our police cars, Leroy and I were both laughing at Tim.

"What was that all about?" I asked.

"Brother, Leroy and me had just finished eating at the Waffle House when we got this call. Now you know I always have to go to the Precinct after I eat at the Waffle House. I love their food, but it goes right through me! We got that domestic call before I could get by the Precinct to drop off that load."

Many years later, I was a shift Lieutenant and Tim was a veteran shift Sergeant. We were the two old guys sitting in Roll Call and telling stories for the entertainment of his young officers. I recounted the story of their Sergeant taking a dump on an Aggravated Domestic Call. His young officers thought that was great.

After the laughing died down, Sergeant Tim looked at me and said, "Yeah, but there is still one part of that story that you don't know. Those people in that double-wide did not have any toilet paper."

"Oh, that is bad," I said. "What did you do?"

"When I was in the Marines, they taught us to improvise, adapt, and overcome," Tim said. "I got a little panicky when I saw there was no toilet paper. But when I looked around the bathroom, I saw a basket full of magazines. I checked them all and found that *Good Housekeeping* had the softest paper. I ripped a few pages out and wadded them up into a ball several times. This got the paper nice and soft and I was able to take care of business."

When Tim's young officers stopped laughing again, I pointed at their Sergeant and said, "That is what a veteran police officer looks like!"

14

Raising Children or Creating Monsters?

I HAVE NOTICED AN interesting trend over the last several years in Law Enforcement. The number of Domestic Disputes between parents and children has gone up drastically. Most of the calls have the parents calling the police because their child is, "out of control." That phrase seems to be used every time we respond to one of these calls. A child does not just wake up one day and become, "out of control." Sure there are some bad kids, but most kids go bad because of bad parenting. What the reader might find interesting is the fact that most of these calls come from predominantly upper middle class neighborhoods. Almost without exception, the homes that we respond to are nice, and in many cases, both parents are in the home.

A few months ago, two of my officers responded to an Aggravated Domestic call in a nice neighborhood near Lawrenceville. I was in the area so I started that way as well. The dispatcher advised that the father was the caller. He had requested the police because his fifteen year old son was destroying the house. I got there first. The fifteen year old was standing out in the front yard. He was a big kid, probably six foot one and at least two hundred and fifty pounds. I asked him what was going on. He said, "I don't know. My dad called for some reason."

We walked into the house so I could talk to his parents. They were a Hispanic family but everyone spoke English. Inside the home, I met Junior's dad. He was a big man himself but not as big as his son. I asked Dad what the problem was. He said, "Take a look at this. Look at what he has done."

In the kitchen, I saw that two kitchen chairs had been smashed to pieces. The kitchen trash can had been dumped out in the middle of the floor. A coffee table in the nearby living room had been destroyed and lay in several broken chunks. I looked at Junior and asked, "What brought this on?"

He shrugged and nodded at his father and said, "He was getting in my face and telling me what to do."

Corporal Mike entered the house. I told him what I knew so far and he went ahead and handcuffed Junior. Mom had been silent up to that point. When the handcuffs went on, she started her third world wail and crying. She said, "Please, don't take my baby away!" *Well, that explains part of the problem*, I thought.

As we spoke with the parents, we found out that Junior had been physically shoving his mother around earlier. He had not gotten physical with his father because he was scared of Dad. Instead, he had broken some of the furniture. Dad also told us that Junior had punched a bunch of holes in the walls upstairs. We had enough to make Domestic Violence charges on Junior, however, because of his age there was a good chance we would have to just write it up and release him back to his parents.

Corporal Mike asked Dad what had brought this on. Dad said that he was a truck driver and was gone several days out of the week. When he had gotten back into town earlier that day, he found out that Junior had been out after midnight several nights that week and would not tell his mother where he had been. Dad had grounded him and set up a curfew for his son. Words were exchanged between Dad and son. Junior was angry at his mother for telling Dad about him being out so late. He was angry at his father for what he felt was too harsh a punishment.

While Corporal Mike was talking to Dad, I asked Mom to show me Junior's room. I followed her up the stairs. There were several fresh holes in the wall going up the steps. I asked Mom if Junior had punched the wall. She said that he had. At the top of the stairs, there was another large hole in the wall. This one was about two feet wide. It looked like he had hit it with something or slammed into it with his shoulder.

I asked Mom which room was Junior's. She said, "He has two bedrooms."

"Why does he have two bedrooms?" I asked.

"Well, he has a lot of things," she answered. "He's an only child so we have an extra bedroom anyway. We let him use both."

She pointed out the two bedrooms. They both had an unmade bed in them. One bedroom had a nice desktop computer and a stereo system. I could see an IPhone and an IPod lying on a table. The closet was bursting with clothes. The other bedroom had a large television, DVD player, Xbox 360 Game System and another closet bursting with clothes.

Mom was still crying. She said, "Please don't take my baby away. He's a good boy."

"He is not a good boy," I told her. "Good boys don't tear up their parent's house or shove their mother around."

"I know he's not good right now. But the rest of the time, he is a good boy," she said.

"Ma'am, he is not a good boy. You have created a monster. You have given him everything he has ever asked for. It doesn't look like you have ever said, "No," to him and this is the result," I told her.

"You are right. So, what do we do now?" she asked. "How do I get him under control?"

"Take all of his stuff away. Get rid of the TV, Xbox, computer, stereo, everything. Take it and give it to Goodwill. Put him in one bedroom and start over. It is going to be hard because he doesn't understand what, "No," means," I told her.

I knew I was wasting my breath. This lady still saw this two hundred and fifty pound guy as her little boy that she loved to spoil. In the end, Corporal Miller wrote up the Domestic Violence report. Because Junior was only fifteen, we could not get authorization to arrest him.

The Juvenile Justice System is by far the weakest link of the Criminal Justice System. If Junior were seventeen, we could arrest him, no questions asked. Because he was under seventeen, we had to call a Juvenile Intake Officer first. Because he had not hurt anyone, we were told release him back to his parents. The Juvenile Court would send them a date in which to appear for a hearing before a Juvenile Judge. Corporal Miller made sure he put the Juvenile Intake Officer's name prominently in the report. That way, if Junior went crazy and really hurt his mother or father, it would be clear that we attempted to do the right thing but were told to leave him there by the Juvenile Intake authorities.

A few weeks later, I responded to another domestic call involving a juvenile and his parents. This time, the caller was the juvenile himself. He turned out to be a very small fifteen year old guy named Demetri. They were a Romanian family. Demetri met me at the entrance to the subdivision. I asked him what the problem was.

He said, "I need you to tell my parents to lighten up. They are too strict. They have grounded me. They took my computer and my phone away. They are ruining my life!"

"And what did you do to bring this on?" I queried.

"It was nothing," Demetri answered. "Nothing. I just borrowed the car one night and drove it around the neighborhood a little. All teenagers do things like that!"

I was really struggling to keep from laughing. I managed to keep the poker face in place and then turned into the Drill Instructor. I got in little Demetri's face and told him that I was disappointed that I had not caught him driving his parent's car without a driver's license. Being grounded would be the least of his concern. His main problem would be getting out of jail.

Demetri's bottom lip started to quiver. I then told him that I was thinking about arresting him for Misuse of 911. I was nose to nose with him now and pouring it on. "I can't believe you called the police for something as stupid as this! You are wasting taxpayer's money because you are such a whiny little boy! I am now going to go talk to your parents and ask them to increase the length of your grounding."

Demtri was bawling now. I left him standing there and drove about two blocks to his parent's house. They were nervous at first, thinking that they had done something wrong. I told them about my little chat with Demetri and let them know that it was clear to me that they were really trying to do the right thing in disciplining him. I told them to keep it up. It was parents like them that would probably make a lasting impact on their son.

Another time, I went with one of my officers on another Aggravated Domestic Call. The mother met us at the door. She was crying. She said that her seventeen year old son, Eric, had pulled a knife on her and threatened to kill her. She had heard him and his twin sister, Shanita, fighting. The Mom saw Eric trying to throw Shanita down the stairs.

While the other officer interviewed Eric, I spoke with Shanita. She had some swelling around one of her eyes. She said that she and her brother fought a lot but that it was never this bad. Tonight, they were arguing over a cell phone. He had punched her in the eye and then tried to throw her down the stairs.

Eric was a little skinny seventeen year old who just shrugged his shoulders when asked about the incident. His mother said that he had called her a number of horrendous names while threatening her with the knife. She told us also that she and the children's father were divorced and that Dad was not around at all.

Eric was arrested and charged with Domestic Violence Charges. While the other officer was getting written statements from Mom and Shanita, I talked to Eric while he sat handcuffed in the backseat of a police car. I asked him what led to this. He said, "I guess I have a problem with anger."

I encouraged him to get some help for his problem. Thankfully, no one was seriously hurt that night, but that is not to say that something worse could not happen in the future. Eric was ultimately put on probation, fined, and required to attend an Anger Management Course. I hope it helped.

As I close this chapter, let me offer a few suggestions to the parents out there. I am drawing on my experience as a parent (my two daughters are both grown and married), as a police officer, and as a pastor. First of all, the primary goal in raising children is not to have "good kids." The goal should be to raise responsible adults that are going to be successful in life. I believe people will approach parenting differently if they focus on helping their children develop skills that will help them become a productive member of society.

A question that I am often asked by new parents is, "How young do you start disciplining children?" I believe that as soon as they start showing defiance, throwing tantrums, and ignoring the "No," of their parents, they need a good dose of loving discipline. Our goal as parents is to mold their will to the point that they will do what we say without us having to raise our voices. Look, I have done my share of yelling at my kids as they were growing up. Parents are human. They lose their tempers and get angry. The intention, however, is still the same: Get them to obey the first time they are told to do something.

Another question that I am often asked is, "Should I spank a young child?" I am a big fan of loving corporal punishment applied when children are willfully disobedient, throwing tantrums, or ignoring a parental, "No." I understand that many parents prefer not to spank. That is fine, as long as they have some method of discipline that works. I found with my children, especially when they were young, spankings worked well. Again, if you do not want to spank your children, that is a personal choice. The main issue is that you have a clearly defined method that you are going to use to discipline your kids. I have always found it difficult to reason with two year olds. A spanking seemed to get my kids' attention.

If children are allowed to disobey, defy, and ignore their parents when they are little, guess what they are going to do as they get older? They are going to continue disobeying, defying, and ignoring you. It will just be over more serious issues. Mold their will while they are young and you probably will not have major issues with your children when they are older.

Another question that I am often asked is this: "Is spanking even legal? Am I going to get arrested if I spank my child?" Most states in America still allow corporal punishment. Get on the internet and check your local laws if you are not sure. This question only becomes an issue if the spanking becomes excessive and injures the child. Remember, the word "discipline" means "to train." Punishment usually comes out of anger. Discipline comes from love. If you are angry, send the child to their room and administer the discipline after you have cooled off. I have been in Law Enforcement for almost thirty years. I have never seen a parent arrested for spanking their child.

What about older children? How should they be disciplined? Remember that our goal as parents is to raise responsible adults. As our children get older, they need to have rules that are clearly spelled out and what the consequences will be if they don't follow them. This is why it is so important that we talk to our children. If they know that they are supposed to be home by eleven o'clock at night and also know that they are going to be grounded if they aren't, there are no surprises.

This is real world training. What is an employer going to do if Johnny can't get out of bed and is consistently late to work at his first job? Their boss is not going to make excuses for them like a permissive parent. The employer is going to fire our little angel because they have not been taught the importance of following rules. One of the worst things that a parent can do is not to follow through on discipline. This sends the message that the parents are weak and don't mean what they say. If our older child is consistently violating the rules that we have put in place, but we are not holding them accountable, we are hurting, not helping them.

There are two last questions in regards to parenting older children that I would like to touch on. These are worst case scenarios. The first is, "When should a parent call the police on their children?" While I discourage getting the police involved in what are usually parental/child issues, I recognize that there are occasions when outside help is needed. I do feel that in ninety eight percent of the calls that I have been on involving a parent and their child, there was no need for the police. But what about the other two percent?

If your child is becoming violent and there is a chance that someone is going to get hurt, call the police. I spoke to a parent recently that told me their seventeen year old has started physically shoving his mother around whenever she tries discipline him in some way. This is never acceptable! This falls under the Family Violence Statute and he can be arrested for this. No parent wants to see their child arrested. At the same time, what kind of parent allows their child to physically abuse them? This child needs to face the consequences of their actions.

Another situation that will probably require police involvement is if your child is involved in illegal activities. I have seen situations where parents knew that their child was selling drugs, doing burglaries, and dealing in stolen property, yet they refused to turn them in. This is a very difficult situation for any parent to be in, but covering for the child will only make the situation more serious. At some point, they are going to get caught or worse. There was a tragic scenario in Gwinnett County a few years ago in which an eighteen year old kid was shot to death at his house in an apparent drug rip-off. His father had known that he was selling drugs out of the house but said he was, "scared to confront him."

The second worst case scenario question is, "What do I do with my eighteen year old that refuses to obey any of our rules and will not listen to me?" My advice is pretty simple. Pack your eighteen year olds' stuff in a box and put the box on the front porch. Then change the locks. This is an actual question I received from a frustrated parent and that was my actual advice. When they turn eighteen, you have fulfilled your legal obligation to them. If they are so much smarter than you, and don't feel that they need to conform to your standards and rules, it is time for them to find another place to live.

I know that this is hard medicine. Dr. James Dobson refers to it as "Tough Love." At the same time, why would any parent want to put up with the stress, frustration, aggravation, and drama that an adult child can provide? I have had more than one parent tell me that this was one of the best moves that they ever made. By putting their problem-causing adult child out of the house, the parent's quality of life has increased dramatically. And in the long run, it is good for the adult child as well. It is forcing them to grow up, take responsibility for their own life, and become a full-fledged adult.

15

Another Vicious Dog

In August of 2010, I was working the afternoon shift. I was leaving the office and heard a Vicious Dog call dispatched to one of my officers. I was only a few miles away so I cleared as his backup. The dispatcher told us that the animal had attacked a Pest Control man that was servicing a neighbor's house. She told us to use caution as the dog had bitten the victim and was still running loose. Animal Control Officers were also on their way to the call. They handle these type of calls, but when the animal is reported to be vicious, the police will be sent as well to protect the unarmed Animal Control Officers.

Officer Jimmy and I got to the neighborhood at about the same time. The victim was a short white guy named Tony. He was limping as he walked over to us. He was wearing a pair of khaki pants and I could see the holes where the dog had bitten through the pants in the area of Tony's right knee. He pulled his pants leg up and showed us two nasty punctures on his leg. One of the holes looked like it might need a couple of stitches.

Tony told us that he was doing a service call at the house his van was parked at. He was about to spray around the outside of the house when a medium sized brown dog charged him from across the street, growling and barking. All Tony had to defend himself with was his pesticide sprayer. He hit the dog over the head with the metal tube when the dog tried to bite him the first time. It bent the tube but did not slow the vicious dog down. It pressed in and bit Tony on the leg. The dog then ran back across the street to the brown frame house where it evidently lived.

While we were talking to Tony, I saw a brown dog come out from under the front porch of the house and run up under a Chevrolet

Suburban in the driveway. Tony said, "That's him. Be careful, Officers. I don't want to see you get bitten."

I assured Tony that that was not going to happen. The dog looked to be some kind of terrier mix and probably weighed about forty or fifty pounds. At that moment, two boys came out of the house where the dog was at. One looked to be about sixteen and the other, maybe ten years old. I yelled across the street so they could hear me, "Hey, is that your dog?"

The boys were Hispanic. The sixteen year old answered me, "Yes, he is our dog."

The older boy reached under the Suburban and grabbed the mutt. I asked him if his parents were at home. The boy said, "No, they are working. What's wrong?"

"Your dog bit someone so I need to talk to your parents. Can you call one of them and ask them to come home?"

It looked like the Mexican boy was holding onto the dog, so I stepped across the road to talk to him without yelling. As soon as I got to the edge of their yard, though, the brown dog pulled away from the boy and started running towards me barking and growling. *And that is the last mistake you will ever make,* I thought. I had to wait until the dog was very close because the two boys were behind him on the driveway. When the dog was about fifteen feet from me, still charging and growling, I quickly drew my Glock 9mm pistol and fired one shot, striking the aggressive dog on the top of the head. He dropped dead at my feet. The silence after the report of the pistol was deafening.

"Is he dead?" the sixteen year old finally asked.

"Yes, son, he is dead. Why didn't you hold onto him?"

"I tried but he just pull away," the boy said.

"Go call your parents and tell them to come home," I told him.

A few minutes later, the boy told me that his mother was on the way home. The Animal Control Officers had arrived and checked the dog. It did not have any tags on showing that it had had its rabies shots. Tony was starting to get worried. He said, "I don't want to have to get rabies shots."

The Animal Control Officer told him, "We will take the dead dog and test it to see if it has rabies. Hopefully, the tests will come back negative and you will not have to get any shots in the stomach."

When the owner of the dog arrived home, I told her what had happened. She did not seem to really care that her dog had bitten someone. The Hispanic woman just kept saying, "I can't believe that you shoot my dog."

The Animal Control Officer asked to see the dog's pen. The Hispanic lady said, "He not stay in pen. He always get out."

When we went into the back yard to see the pen, we were surprised to see a mother Boxer and several puppies living in the pen in squalid conditions. The pen was made out of chicken wire so it was no surprise that the dead dog had escaped so easily. It was also obvious that these other dogs were really not being taken care of. The Animal Control Officer ended up writing the woman eight citations. Three of them were for Vicious Dog, Unrestrained Dog, and No Rabies Tags for the one that I had shot. The other five tickets were for the dogs in the backyard and their poor living conditions. In all, the lady was looking at about fifteen hundred dollars in fines.

Now I know that I probably sound pretty cavalier about killing this dog, these people's pet. I will confess that I did not lose any sleep at all that night. Here is the way that I look at it. By killing that vicious dog, I saved some little child in that neighborhood from getting mauled. The idea of some kid having to get rabies shots did not set well with me. Some people should not own dogs. If they really want a pet, maybe they should just get a goldfish.

16

Alligator on the Loose

I HAVE HANDLED OR been a part of a lot of weird calls over the years. The day that I met the alligator in Dacula was by far one of the strangest. Dacula is a small town in the still predominantly rural area of the East Precinct in Gwinnett County. To my knowledge, there are no wild alligators in Gwinnett County. We have no swamps to speak of and it is just not alligator country. I was more than a little surprised when I heard my friend, Lieutenant Greg, call over the police radio for assistance in his neighborhood about a loose alligator.

It was a sunny, spring afternoon and Greg was on his way home. I had recently taken his place as the second shift watch commander at the East Precinct when he took an administrative assignment. As he was pulling into his subdivision after work, he was flagged down by two ladies who had been walking their small dogs. They told Greg that they had been near the clubhouse next to the neighborhood pool when their dogs had started barking at something in the bushes. They had gotten a glimpse of what they said was a large alligator lurking in the bushes.

I was nearby so I responded with Sergeant Randy and two zone cars. I did not really believe that there was an alligator hiding in the bushes. *Maybe it was just a big lizard*, I thought. *Or, maybe someone captured a baby alligator in Florida and brought it home as a pet.* When I pulled up and got out of my police car, Lieutenant Greg was talking to the ladies who had flagged him down. They were holding their little dogs, talking excitedly, and pointing at the bushes about fifty feet away. I heard one of them say, "He's huge! I thought he was going to eat my dog."

The other lady said, "Yeah, and it was making these hissing noises when it came out from the bushes. It is back in there now hiding."

I looked over at the bushes they were talking about. It was a tall, thick hedgerow that ran along the side of the clubhouse. I saw a few small openings every couple of feet. Greg walked over to me smiling. He said, "Well, there is something in there. I know these ladies and they are not the type to exaggerate or make something like this up."

We decided to walk over to the bushes and see what we could see. That would determine what we would do next. Greg went and got his shotgun out of his police car. That looked like a good idea, just in case. I got my patrol rifle out of my patrol car and chambered a round. I set the selector on "safe." Sergeant Randy had his camera out. The three of us started across the fifty feet of open space to the hedgerow. We were still about twenty feet from the hedgerow when I saw the bushes start moving. A six foot long alligator came strolling out, right towards us. We made a hasty retreat back to the parking lot and the 'gator turned left and walked towards the front of the clubhouse. He was easily big as me. I am six foot two and weighed about two hundred and forty pounds at the time. This alligator probably weighed around two hundred and fifty pounds.

An Animal Control Officer pulled into the parking lot. Nicole got out of her truck and grabbed her pole with the noose on it. She was kind of on the small side. I wondered if she had any experience in catching 'gators. I am guessing that was not covered in her training. The two zone officers I had there with me were Angela and Wendy. To their credit, they were ready to do whatever I told them. The 'gator stopped in front of the building and glared at us. He did not look particularly aggressive, but how do you know if an alligator is agitated? I did not want to shoot it except as a last resort. We were surrounded by houses and I did not want to risk a ricochet. But, how do you capture an alligator?

Animal Control Officer Nicole had her metal pole out. These are long and have a wire noose on the end. They use these for snaring stray dogs. She had an extra one and Sergeant Randy took it. He told Officer Wendy to get her riot shield out. Nicole said she was going to try and snare the 'gator and asked us to cover her. Greg and I still had our long guns out. The plastic riot shield that Wendy held might slow the alligator down if he charged us.

The animal had stopped on the sidewalk in front of the clubhouse and appeared to be sunning himself. He was not paying much attention to us or our preparations. Nicole was able to slip up behind him and slip the wire noose around his neck. The 'gator did not like that and started hissing. He attempted to swing around towards Nicole. Wendy had her shield on the ground and blocked the alligator's progress. Sergeant Randy then slipped his noose around the animal's neck as well. The 'gator really started struggling to get away. He was hissing and squirming. It was all Randy and Nicole could do to hold on. They stood on the animal's tail in an effort to keep him from jerking the poles out of their hands. Now, the animal appeared to be agitated.

About this time, the Animal Control Supervisor, Scott, pulled up. He jumped out of his truck and hurried over to where we were at. Without any warning, he jumped on the alligator's back and grabbed its snout with both hands. Very calmly, he asked, "Does anybody have some duct tape?"

Greg said he thought he had some in his car and went to get it. All of the police officers there were staring in amazement at Scott. I had seen Steve Irwin, "The Crocodile Hunter," on TV many times. The History Channel's, *Swamp People*, shows people wrestling with big alligators every week. The idea of jumping on the 'gator's back and grabbing his snout was comparable to me to licking my finger and putting it in an electrical outlet. Something bad was going to happen! Scott just kept sitting on the beast that was squirming to get away. The two wire nooses around his neck helped keep him in place. When Lieutenant Greg returned with a roll of duct tape, Scott instructed him to tear off lengths of about eighteen inches. Greg tore off the strip of tape. Now Scott said, "Okay, now wrap it around his snout while I hold it closed."

Greg looked at Scott, as if in disbelief, but he did what he was told, quickly wrapping the duct tape around the alligator's long snout. "Good. Now, let's do it one more time, just to be sure," Scott said.

Greg quickly wrapped another long strip of tape around the animal's snout. With the 'gator's mouth taped shut, Scott released the snout and slid backwards, towards its tail. He took the duct tape from Greg and ran it underneath the animal, taping his short front legs to its body. He slid back onto the tail and repeated the process with the rear legs. Now, the alligator was immobilized thanks to man's other best friend, duct tape. I think we all exhaled at the same time. I had been waiting to see Scott lose a finger or a hand. Thankfully, he still had all his appendages.

Nicole opened one of the side compartments on her Animal Control truck. She, Scott, and a couple of police officers hoisted the animal into the truck. I asked Scott, "So, what do you do with a captured alligator?"

"That is a good question," he said. "As far as I know, this is the first one that we have ever captured in Gwinnett. We will call The Department of Natural Resources and see if they want it. My best guess is that they will take him down to a swamp in South Georgia and let him go."

The last I heard, our alligator friend was released into a South Georgia swamp. He was enjoying himself and doing whatever 'gators do in the wild. And, no, we never found out how he ended up, hanging out at the pool in a nice neighborhood in Gwinnett County.

17

The Cop and the Kitty

It was a busy afternoon in the Norcross area. The radio chatter was constant as domestic calls, car accidents, burglaries, and suspicious activity calls were being dispatched to the zone officers. I was a Sergeant in the Tactical Operations Section at the time and my squad of officers was working in the Norcross area that day. Normally, we would not respond to dispatched calls. We were expected to be proactive, looking for and investigating criminal activity. At the same time, we could all hear over the police radio that it was an unusually busy shift. A couple of my guys were already helping out by jumping some of the dispatched calls to give the zone officers a breather.

I then heard the dispatcher call the Shift Sergeant over the radio. She said, "I have a Burglary in Progress/Home Invasion pending. The suspects are two black males and are armed with automatic weapons. They are still inside the apartment at this time. All units are busy on other calls. What do you advise?"

It is a frustrating feeling when there is a serious call pending and you do not have anyone to go to it. I had been in that Sergeant's shoes before. Normally, the Shift Sergeant would start for the call himself, but in this case, he was out on a car accident with one of his officers helping to direct traffic.

Before the Shift Sergeant could answer the dispatcher, two of my officers said that they were clear and enroute to the call. Officer Michele and Officer Josh were actually just up the street from the apartment complex where this was occurring. I cleared on the call as well. I was about ten minutes away but the serious nature of the call required that a supervisor respond. This was the type of call that really required four to six officers to respond but we just did not have them available at the moment.

There was really no way for two officers to safely handle this call and I was concerned for their safety. The dispatcher had told us that the suspects were two black males, one of whom had a machine gun. The caller was evidently nearby in the apartment complex and was watching the apartment, because they could see that the suspects were still inside the apartment.

Josh and Michele got to the apartment complex within minutes of being dispatched. A zone unit had just finished up the car wreck that he was working and said that he was responding as well. The apartment that was being robbed was upstairs on the second level. Michele went to the rear to cover the back door. She drew her pistol and took cover behind a tree.

Josh started up the stairs as the other police car came screeching to a halt in the parking lot. Josh and the zone officer slowly approached the apartment door with their pistols out. They could hear loud voices speaking Spanish inside the apartment. A large percentage of the residents who lived in this area were illegal Hispanics. The officers had a choice to make. Should they approach and knock on the door? Should they cover off and shout out a challenge for the perps to come out? Should they try and locate a phone number for the apartment and call, trying to make contact with someone inside?

Josh elected to approach the door. It was probably the best choice that they had. The other officer stood back several feet, covered off behind a corner, with his pistol aimed at the door. Josh approached from the side so that if the bad guys shot through the door, he would not be hit. Officer Josh, like so many of us, spoke some Spanish. If you work in that area, you have to be able communicate, at least on a basic level.

He knocked loudly on the door and yelled, "Policia! Abrir la puerta!"

Meanwhile, Officer Michele was behind the apartment building watching the back door. She had a good cover position behind a tree and had her pistol in a low ready position. It had been several minutes since she and Josh had split up and she had gone to cover the rear. She was not sure what was going on at the front door. As she watched the building, she noticed a little gray kitten walking around near her feet.

Michele and her husband, also a police officer, are both extreme pet lovers. I say extreme because I do not think that either one of them have ever met a stray that they did not like. Their home has been compared to a petting zoo. This kitten looked to be only a week or two old. Michele seemed interesting and the kitten started rubbing up against her as she was watching the back of the apartment.

At Josh's knock on the front door, all voices and noise inside ceased. After a few seconds, they could hear movement inside the apartment and some excited voices chattering in both English and Spanish. Josh reached down and turned the door knob. The door was unlocked. He made eye contact with his backup officer. Josh pushed open the door into the apartment.

The officers swept their eyes over the interior of the living room, just inside the front door. Three Hispanic women and two Hispanic men were sitting on the couch and armchairs. They looked scared and Josh could see that their hands were tied up in front of them. When the people saw the police, they did not say anything right away. One of the males, who was sitting in an armchair directly across from the front door, looked at the officers and motioned to his right, with his head. The officers could hear the sound of footsteps stomping through the kitchen and then the sound of the back door coming open.

As the kitten continued to rub up against Officer Michele's legs, Michele saw another police car racing into the parking lot. It was a second zone officer. As he jumped out of his police car, Michele motioned for him to come and join her in the back. At that moment, the back door of the apartment came flying open and the two suspects came running out onto the second floor landing.

Michele and her backup officer immediately pointed their pistols at the two men. "Get your hands up!" Michele barked at the two men. She saw the larger of the two men toss a big gun to the side. The two men realized that there was nowhere for them to go. They threw their hands into the air.

"Get down on the ground!" Michele yelled again.

When Josh heard the back door opening and Michele yelling from outside, he and his backup officer rushed through the apartment. This was a calculated risk. If any of the perps had hung back, the two officers could find themselves in a gunfight in the enclosed space of the apartment. Josh was betting that the perps had tried to make a hasty retreat when they heard the police at the front door.

As the officers were running through the apartment, Josh heard Michele on the police radio saying that the suspects were coming out the back door. When the two officers got through the kitchen to where the back door was standing open, they slowed down. They did not want to go running outside and take a chance on getting shot by fellow officers. Josh saw the two suspects on the small landing next to the stairs that led to the ground level. The bad guys were in the process of getting down on their knees and then laying facedown, as Michele had ordered. Josh noticed a nasty looking gun lying to the side of the perps.

Josh and his backup officer took control. "Put your hands behind your back," Josh ordered.

As his backup covered the perps with his pistol, Josh quickly handcuffed and then thoroughly searched both of them. They did not have any other weapons. The bad guys did have jewelry and several hundred dollars in their pockets. It was later determined that all of this had been taken from the victims inside the apartment. Josh advised over the police radio that they were okay and that they had two suspects in custody.

I had finally managed to fight my way through the afternoon traffic and pulled my police truck up to where their police cars were parked. I was running up the stairs to the apartment as Josh was saying that they had the two bad guys in custody. As I entered the apartment, all five of the victims were still sitting with their hands tied. I checked on Josh and the other officers. Michele and her backup had come up the stairs to assist. One of the suspects was a really big guy. He probably weighed over three hundred pounds. They could not get him to his feet on the small deck because he was so big. They actually had to slide the fat guy down the stairs slowly. When they got him to the bottom, there was enough room to help get him to his feet.

The bad guys were secured in separate police cars. The gun that the big guy had had was a Cobray M-11 9mm pistol. It was not really a machine gun, but it did look kind of menacing. It only fired in semi-automatic mode but it had a thirty round magazine in it. The M-11 also had a round in the chamber and the safety was off. It was ready to go. Thankfully, Officer Michele had a good cover position in the back of the apartment and was able to get the drop on the bad guys.

Back in the apartment, we cut the shoe laces that the victims were tied up with. *Shoe laces? Were these perps that bad or could they just not afford a roll of duct tape?* I wondered. Because we had five victims, none of whom spoke English, and two suspects in custody that were probably good for more than just this one robbery, I contacted the Detective Division and asked for their help. Since no one had been hurt, there really was not much of a crime scene. The Detective Sergeant had us load the perps and the victims into several police cars and bring them up to Headquarters for interviews. The gun, stolen property and money, and the shoe laces were secured as evidence. We also took photographs of the inside of the apartment.

As we were getting the bad guys, victims, and evidence secured inside the apartment, Officer Michele walked up to me. She said, "Hey Sarge, do you want to see something cute?"

She turned sideways and showed me her side cargo pocket on her utility pants. The little head of a kitten poked up over the side. I could hear it meowing.

"Where did you find that?" I asked.

She told me the story of the kitty playing around her feet as she and the other officer took down the armed robbers. "So what are you going to do with it?" I asked.

"We will try and find him a home," she answered. "We have a vet that will neuter him for free and then we will try and adopt him out."

During the interviews with the suspects and the victims, the detectives found out that the apartment that we had been at was being used as a brothel. The three girls were prostitutes and the two guys were customers. Everything took an interesting spin when the detectives were interviewing the suspects. We had caught them in the act of committing the robbery so there was no point in denying it. They both gave full video taped confessions. The curve ball was that one of the bad guys said that one of the prostitutes had set the robbery up. She knew the perp from a previous "business" transaction and had gotten them to do the robbery. They had tied her up too, but were planning on splitting the money with her later.

After the interviews, the detectives secured a search warrant for the apartment and went back to the location to serve it. They found some cocaine in one of the bedrooms and some more money that the perps had missed. When it was all said and done, the two black guys were charged with a host of serious crimes, including Armed Robbery. The prostitute that set it up was charged with Conspiracy and was deported after she served a short jail sentence. The other two prostitutes and the two guys that happened to be there were charged with Drug Possession and some misdemeanor charges related to Prostitution.

I did not see Officer Michele any more that day. The next morning, I asked her about her kitten. She said, "You are going to love this. He pooped in my pocket. And he had diarrhea. I thought that I was never going to get my pocket cleaned out!"

So, sometimes when you do a good deed, you still get crapped on. Although, I'm not sure saving a kitten is really a good deed. The real good deed that day was capturing some dangerous criminals. The lucky kitty just happened to be in the right place at the right time.

18

Weird Stuff

My first assignment after I got promoted to Sergeant was at our West Precinct, near Norcross. This has usually been our busiest precinct and the area that contained the greatest saturation of drugs, gangs, and violent crime. The first six months that I was a Sergeant, I was on Day Shift. When an opportunity to transfer to the Midnight Shift came, I took it. Most of my career had been spent on the third shift and I acclimated to it quickly.

My third night on the night shift, Officer James approached me after Roll Call. "Hey Sarge, tonight is the night that we do a walk through of the El Imperio Club. Do you want to join us? It should be packed tonight and the women there are gorgeous!"

The area that the West Precinct covered contained our county's largest concentration of Hispanics, many of whom were in the country illegally. There were a multitude of clubs that catered to them, as well as to many other nationalities, throughout our district. Because of the increasing number of fight calls, assaults, and drug complaints coming from these establishments, officers had been directed to pick one or two of these clubs a night to walk through and show some police presence. This gave the officers an excuse to check and make sure that the establishment had all the proper business and alcohol permits. The servers are also required to have a permit, issued by the County, to serve alcohol. Many of the employees at these clubs were here illegally and, of course, could not get a serving permit. This usually meant citations for the manager and an arrest of the illegal server. We also knew that a lot of drugs were being sold at these clubs and we did what we could to ruin the drug dealer's business.

When Officer James said that they were checking the El Imperio and asked me to join them, I quickly agreed. The El Imperio was by far the biggest Hispanic club in the area. The building was also the gaudiest. The large dragon head on the front of the building made it a unique landmark.

I pulled into the parking lot of the Hispanic club at one in the morning. The parking lot was packed and it looked like the place was hopping. Four other police cars pulled in and we parked in the back. Officers never checked a club by themselves. For a club this big, five officers was about right. As we were walking to the door, I commented on the number of tall women in short skirts that were either coming or going to the club. For some reason, my comment made a couple of the officers laugh.

The Latin music was loud and the cigarette smoke was thick in the air as we entered the club. There were a few tables scattered around the place, but most of the interior was taken up by the dance floor. Ten or twelve couples were currently slow dancing on the floor. *Those really are some big, tall women,* I thought. Just inside the front door, seated at a table, a young couple was engaged in some heavy kissing. They both turned and looked at us as we came through the door and I realized that they were both men! One of them had on a skirt, blouse, makeup, and jewelry but there was no mistaking his Adams apple and the five o'clock shadow on his face.

Another glance at the couples on the dance floor confirmed that they too were all men. No wonder those "girls" looked so big! The four officers that were with me had been watching for my reaction and were all laughing at the horrified expression on my face. Officer James spoke up and said, "Sarge, I forgot to tell you that Thursday nights here are Mexican Transvestite Nights."

"Yeah, I'm sure you forgot. It is easy for something like that to slip your mind," I said laughing. I pointed at the two men that were kissing when we came in. "That is disgusting!"

I don't know if the two sweethearts understood English or not, but I think they understood the tone of my voice. They each slid their chair backwards and maintained the six inch rule until we left. By now I realized that the guys had pulled a great gag on me. I was the new Sergeant on the shift and they had to mess with me. I was over my initial shock by now and I couldn't help but laugh. "I bet you bastards think you are pretty funny, huh? Well, you got me! That was one of the best pranks I've ever had pulled on me. Now, let's go check their permits."

We did not find any violations. We did find four Mexican guys in a closet putting on women's underwear. They actually squealed like girls when we opened the door. "Aren't Mexican guys supposed to be, you know, macho?" I asked Officer James.

"I don't know, Sarge. I think these guys are missing that *machismo* gene."

A few years later, I was again working the overnight shift as a Sergeant, this time assigned to Special Operations. I was part of a Robbery Task Force trying to cut down on the rash of armed robberies that we were having in the Norcross area. We were having as many as five or six robberies a night. Most of the victims were drunk Hispanics staggering home from a bar. They were an easy target for the numerous groups of armed robbers that were working that area. The robbers would usually just drag the victim into the shadows and demand their money and cell phone. If the victim resisted, they were beaten, shot, or stabbed.

Officer Josh came over the police radio and said that he was out on two suspicious females. He described them as, "one with brown hair, one with blond hair, and both wearing short skirts and high heels." I was nearby so I cleared as his backup unit. It was two o'clock in the morning. These had to be working girls, prostitutes, to be out in that part of town walking around dressed like that, at that hour of the night. As I pulled up with Officer Josh, so did three other marked squad cars and an undercover car. I think his radio traffic about the "short skirts," got some of the guys' attention. They were destined to be disappointed.

As Josh walked over to me, I could see that he was blushing and he had a silly, "I got fooled grin" on his face. The two hookers were standing about twenty feet away with their backs to us. Josh was smiling apologetically. "I'm sorry, Sarge. I thought that they were girls."

I did not understand what he was implying. "What do you mean?"

"They are both guys," he told me.

"You have got to be kidding," I said. "They both look good from the rear."

"I know," said Josh. "They had me fooled until I got out to talk with them."

Two of our Vice Detectives, John and Kathleen, were in the undercover car. The male detective, John, was talking to the two streetwalkers like he thought they were women. As I walked up, he was telling the blond that "she" had pretty hair. Even up close, they were pretty convincing. The brunette had a wig on, but the blond had long hair that he/she had spent a lot of time on. The blond said his/her name was "America." America spoke some English but the brunette didn't. Detective John said, "Where do you get your hair done? It is so pretty!"

America did not know what to make of this attention from the big, white, plain clothes cop. America said, in heavily accented English, "I'm a guy."

John feigned shock and said, "No! I never would have known."

John's female partner, Kathleen, just rolled her eyes. Officer Josh checked the two guy/girl wannabes on the warrant computer and did not find anything. We did not have any charges on them. It is not illegal to dress up like a girl and we had no evidence that they were soliciting for sex, even though it was obvious that that is exactly what they were doing.

We did not find out until later that America and her/his partner were actually robbery suspects. They were picking up drunk Mexicans at some of the local clubs and going back to the victim's apartment. Either before or after the dirty deed was done, America and friend would hit the poor guy over the head and take all his money.

Very few of these Mexicans were reporting the crime. First of all, they were embarrassed that they had possibly been involved in a sex act with a guy. Secondly, who would believe that they were robbed by an attractive blond in a short skirt, especially one that was really a guy and was named, "America?"

19

Prostitutes, Midgets, and Drugs

Busting a Mexican Bordello

PROBABLY THE BEST POSITION that ever I held in the police department was as a Sergeant in the Crime Suppression Unit. Crime Suppression was part of the Special Operations Section. Officers that are assigned to the CSU are some of the best officers in the Department. They are highly motivated and experienced. Many of the officers in the CSU were also assigned to the SWAT team, but all of us received extra training in small unit tactics, vehicle takedowns, gangs, and drugs. Being a Sergeant in the CSU was like being a player/coach for an All-Star team.

Crime Suppression's mission was multi-faceted. We spent a lot of time tracking down armed robbers and other violent criminals. While I was part of the unit, we took down a number of robbery crews that were preying mostly on Hispanic victims. Another major area that we concentrated on was street-level drug sales. We used informants, undercover surveillance, and other techniques to take down a number of drug operations. I discussed some of these in *Street Cop*.

The CSU also worked very closely with our Criminal Investigations Division, and specifically the Narcotics, Robbery, and Vice Units. Once or twice a week I would get a call from a Detective Sergeant asking us to help them find someone or to help them serve a warrant.

I had just gotten to the office one afternoon when my boss, Lieutenant Greg, stopped in to let me know that we were going to be helping the Vice Unit raid some Mexican brothels. It was going to be a fun night! We came to work at five in the afternoon. The briefing with Vice was scheduled for seven o'clock. I told all the guys to go grab some dinner and then meet at the West Precinct for the seven o'clock briefing.

When I walked into the briefing room, I was surprised to see that it was packed with uniformed officers and detectives. As the briefing started it became apparent that this was a big investigation. The lead investigator was a big white guy. He was dressed like a biker, with long hair, a beard, several piercings, and numerous tattoos. He was clad in blue jeans, a Harley Davidson t-shirt, a leather vest, and a Jack Daniels ball cap.

The Detective told us that we were going to be taking down three Mexican brothels at the same time. They were all controlled by the same people. Each one of the brothels was supposed to have a security element present to protect the girls. Drugs and prostitution go hand in hand and it was expected that we would find some narcotics at the different locations. We would be serving simultaneous search warrants at the three brothels. By hitting them all at the same time, there would be no opportunity for them to alert each other and then disappear.

One of the locations was going to be dealt with by the West Precinct's Criminal Response Team. Each precinct has at least one CRT Team. The CRT teams do the same kinds of things that the Crime Suppression Unit does. The biggest difference is that the CRT's only focus on the area that their precinct covers. Crime Suppression covers the entire county, is a much bigger operation, and has more resources. The second brothel was going to be handled by a group of Vice Investigators.

When Investigator Biker turned to me and my guys he said, "I am giving you Crime Suppression guys the tough one. Usually, we don't have any resistance when we take down brothels. If we do have any problems, though, it will be at the one you will be at. The pimp there is supposed to be a pretty tough guy and is known to sometimes carry a gun. He got shot in the butt last year when some guys tried to rob him. You can't miss identifying him. He's a midget."

I raised my hand. "Excuse me. I must have misheard you. I thought you said that the tough pimp, who carries a gun, was a Mexican midget?"

By now, everyone in the room was snickering at the visual that they were imagining. The Detective said, "That's right. He has a reputation for being a pretty dangerous character."

This only increased the laughter. Detective Biker paused for the laughter to subside. "If he is armed, make sure you aim low." A new wave of laughter erupted. We all knew the potential for danger was there, but this also had comedy written all over it.

The plan was for six of the Crime Suppression officers to pile into two unmarked cars. The other CSU officers would be in their marked units. The brothel that we were hitting was in an apartment complex. The unmarked cars would go in first and park in front of the apartment. The six of us would bail out and rush the apartment. The marked units and two of the Vice Detectives would come pulling in about thirty seconds later. CSU officers would make entry, clear the apartment, and secure everyone inside. The detectives would then come in and execute their Search Warrant.

After the briefing, I made the assignments for who would be in the unmarked cars and who would be in their marked units. The marked units would be needed to transport prisoners later. It was time to go. Three of the six CSU officers in the unmarked cars would be carrying a rifle or a submachine gun. The rest of us would be armed with our pistols. The apartment that my group was going to was on the ground floor, which made things a bit easier. Stairs were never any fun to negotiate when you were in a hurry.

We arrived at the rundown apartment complex in Norcross. It was occupied almost exclusively by Hispanics. The two undercover vehicles that we were in were a minivan and a quad cab pickup truck. They did not attract any attention as they stopped in front of the apartment building. When all of the big, heavily armed, uniformed police officers jumped out and ran up to the door of the target apartment, everyone was paying attention. The marked units pulled in right behind us. The Vice Detectives were on the scene quickly as well.

As we approached the apartment, we saw a Hispanic male sitting in a lawn chair a few feet from the door that we were going to. A Hispanic woman was standing next to him and they were talking. When the man saw us, he jumped up and tried to get to the apartment. Two of my guys grabbed him and the woman and took them to the ground where they were handcuffed and quickly searched. Neither was armed, but it was obvious that the male was the outside lookout for the brothel.

The two Vice Detectives ran up to where we were at. They were wearing jeans and t-shirts. They had on body armor and raid vests that were marked "Police" in large letters. They were also wearing black hoods over their faces. Only their eyes were showing. The hoods protected their identity because they often worked in undercover roles. The man and the woman on the ground looked up with big eyes as the two men wearing masks and carrying guns came running up and held them down.

The search warrant that we were serving was a "Knock" warrant. That meant we had to knock on the door and announce our presence. If the occupants did not answer the door within a couple of minutes, we had our metal ram to smash in the door. The problem with "Knock" warrants was that it gave the occupants time to dispose of evidence. This usually meant flushing drugs down the toilet.

We lucked out at this apartment. When we got to the door, we noticed that it wasn't closed all the way. It was like they were inviting us in! The lead officer knocked on the partially open door and yelled, "Police! Search Warrant!" Since the door was already open, we stepped right into the living room.

The first person that we saw was the Mexican midget pimp. He was standing in the living room. As we were bursting in with our guns at the low ready, the little guy looked like he was going to faint. He did not speak English but he understood the spirit behind, "Get your hands up!" He tried to comply but his arms were short and would not go up very high. He was quickly handcuffed and searched. Because his arms were so short, we had to use two sets of handcuffs to get him secured.

While two officers were securing the little pimp, the rest of us cleared the apartment. There was a Mexican woman in the bedroom getting dressed. She appeared to be in her mid-thirties. We could hear the shower running in the bathroom. As soon as she had her clothes on, she was handcuffed and taken out to the living room. There was a guy in the shower who had just partaken of the woman's services. He was ordered out of the shower and told to dry off and get his clothes on. He did not speak English either, but some forms of communication are universal. After he was handcuffed, he was also taken out to the living room.

Search Warrants are not Arrest Warrants. We had five people handcuffed and sitting in the living room: the lookout, the girl that was with him, the pimp, the prostitute, and the customer. Even though they were handcuffed, they were not under arrest yet. The legal term is "Investigative Detention." They were being detained until the Search

Warrant was executed. That would determine whether or not the handcuffs came off. Search Warrants specify what they are looking for. This one said that it was looking for evidence related to the crimes of prostitution and illegal drugs.

The bedroom contained quite a bit of evidence related to prostitution. The Vice Investigator found a jumbo-sized box of unused condoms. The investigator also made a very nasty discovery on a small table next to the bed. There was a stack of twelve used condoms, each one covered by a paper towel. They were layered with paper towels between them. We found out later that this was how the girl got paid for services. She would turn in the used condoms as proof of how much "work" she had done for the day. The twelve used condoms meant that this working girl had had a busy shift! Aside from the condoms, the bedroom also contained deluxe sized containers of personal lubricant and lotion.

The hall closet contained some small baggies of powder cocaine. The quantity of cocaine was not that much, but the fact that it was in ten separate baggies allowed the detectives to charge them with Possession with Intent to Distribute Cocaine. After they finished searching the apartment, one of the investigators interviewed each of the suspects that we had detained. After the interviews, everyone was arrested except the girl who was with the lookout outside. We could not establish that she lived there. The lookout, the midget pimp, and the prostitute all lived in the apartment. The customer had the bad luck of picking that day to visit the brothel.

We escorted the four suspects out to the police cars. I saw an officer open his back door and motion for the handcuffed midget to get in. The little guy looked up at the backseat and laughed. It took two officers to pick him up and put him in the police car.

After we released the other girl, she quickly disappeared. A neighbor came out and thanked us for shutting the bordello down. She lived right across the hall and said that she had small children. She asked in broken English, "Why you no take other girl? She the main girl there." Evidently, the girl that we had released was the main prostitute. It must have been her off day.

20

Most Embarrassing Moments

If you do anything long enough, you are bound to make a fool of yourself occasionally. I have had my share of goof ups over my long career. Fortunately, most of them were not serious and the only injury was to my ego. Thankfully, with a little rest and massage, the ego bounces back to health pretty quickly.

When I was a very young police officer, I was working a quiet Sunday morning on Day Shift. I stopped at a convenience store in Norcross to use the restroom and get a cup of coffee. My plan was to go to the nearby park and meet Officer Jay. We would sit in the shade, read the newspaper and drink our coffee until we got a call for service.

I walked into the convenience store and asked the Pakistani clerk if I could use the restroom. Achmed handed me a key attached to long piece of wood. He said the restroom was behind the store. I walked out back and saw that the restrooms were actually in a separate building behind the main store. When I got in the restroom, I was really glad I did not have to do anything but pee. It was nasty and smelly. *What's the point of keeping the restroom locked and tying the key to a two by four if you aren't ever going to clean it?* I wondered.

After I finished up inside the restroom, I turned the door knob to let myself out. The door was locked. The lock was on the inside of the door but no matter which way I turned it, the heavy metal door would not open. There were no windows in the restroom. *This must be what it feels like to be in prison*, I thought. I banged on the door for a few minutes but no one came to my rescue. There was no way that Achmed could hear me from where he was at inside the store. He could not even see the restrooms from his vantage point in the front of the store. This was before we were all issued walkie-talkies or cell phones had even been invented. If I had had a radio, I would have just called Officer Jay and had him come help me. As it was, it looked like I was locked in this funky smelling restroom until somebody missed me.

What do you do when you are trapped in a disgusting restroom? There is no place to sit. You don't want to touch anything. You can only hold your breath for so long. I banged on the door some more, but to no avail. I gave the metal door a really good kick but it did not budge. Then I noticed that the hinges were on the inside. The door opened inward. I reached in my pocket and pulled out my folding knife. It took a few minutes, but I was able to pry all three of the hinge bolts out of the door. I was covered with grease by the time I was done, but I was almost free.

After I got the bolts out of the hinges, I just pulled the door loose, picked it up, and set it in the corner of the restroom. I tried to wash the grease off of my hands but, of course, there was no soap in the dispenser. I cleaned up as best I could and then took Achmed his key. I told him what had happened and he apologized profusely. He looked very worried. My guess is that in Pakistan, the police probably kill you for less than that.

I finally got my coffee and met up with Jay at the park. "Are you okay?" he asked. "I was beginning to get worried. Did something you ate not agree with you?"

After I told him the story and he quit laughing, I became known as the guy who needed a backup when he went to the restroom. Achmed got the door fixed by the next time I stopped in at his store. After that, he would never accept any money from me for coffee or snacks. I think he was still worried that I might kill him.

Most people remember the famous "wardrobe malfunction" that took place during the Halftime Show at Super Bowl XXXVIII, between Janet Jackson and Justin Timberlake. I had a wardrobe malfunction of my own once. Thankfully, it was not on live television, but it was still embarrassing.

Officer Marco and I were working the midnight shift near Norcross. We received a burglar alarm to a business in an industrial area. This business had been broken into twice in the last month so there was a very good possibility that this would be a good alarm. We both got to the location at the same time. The front of the business was secure. There was a six foot, chain link fence that prevented us from checking the rear of the location.

Marco pulled his police car right up to the fence. He then climbed up on the hood and went over the chain link fence. "What are you doing?" I asked. "You know I don't do fences!"

He said, "We have to check the rear. This might be a burglary."

I hated to climb fences. My philosophy was that if the business owner put a fence up, they did not want us checking the rear of the business. There is no easy way to get over a fence and I have never made a practice of climbing over them. If the business owner really wanted us to check the rear of his business, then the burglar alarm monitoring company could call him, wake him up, and have him come open the gate.

With Marco already over the fence, though, I found myself in a quandary. I really did not want to climb a six foot high fence. At the same time, I did not want to leave my brother officer unprotected as he checked the rear of the business. I went over the fence. Or at least I tried to. I got up on the hood of his police car, and swung my leg over the top of the fence. That is when I had my "wardrobe malfunction." My pants split right down the middle of my crotch. I was already committed so I went ahead and climbed down the other side of the fence.

Marco saw what had happened and started laughing at me. I had a few thoughts that I shared with him and then we checked the rear of the business. It was secure. That was good, but how were we going to get out of the locked fence? We went ahead and just climbed back over the way that we had come. It was a bit harder this time because we did not have a car to climb onto but we both managed to get back to the other side. I was nervous going back over, though. With the crotch of my pants gone, I was pretty exposed and I did not want to hurt myself.

We had cleared the call but it was still early in the shift and I had a serious uniform issue that I had to deal with. I lived about thirty minutes away so going home was not really an option. We were already running short handed that night and if I went home to change pants that would leave the shift an officer short for at least an hour.

The City of Norcross has their own small police department, as do several of the other municipalities in Gwinnett County. I have always made it a policy to stay on good terms with these departments. You never know when you are going to be fighting for your life and they are coming to back you up. I want them rushing to get to me, not thinking, "Oh, yeah. That county officer is a prick. I'll drive slow and get there when I get there."

Norcross Police Department's headquarters was nearby so I stopped in. Their dispatcher was a girl that I had talked to a few times. I explained my situation to her and asked if she had any ideas. She came to the rescue with three safety pins. I went into the restroom and very carefully pinned myself together. It wasn't perfect but it got me through the night.

I have talked about some of my encounters with vicious dogs in both *Street Cop* books. In those stories, I made out okay. I had another situation with a dog that took me a while to live down. I was dispatched to a Disturbance/Fight call at a house near Snellville. The dispatcher said that a neighbor was calling about yelling that was coming from this address. It sounded like there were multiple people fighting in the front yard. When I pulled up and parked near the house, there was no one visible. There were several cars in the driveway and street and I could hear music playing inside. *It looks like a pretty tame party*, I thought.

When I rang the doorbell, a very drunk blond girl opened the door. When I asked her if everything was okay, she managed to say, "Great! Everything is great!" When I told her that we had gotten a Disturbance Call at her house, she said, "I don't live here. This isn't my house because I don't live here. I'm just visiting here, but I don't live here."

If drunk people knew how stupid they sounded, I thought, *they would just keep drinking.*

"Can you go get the owner of house for me, since you don't live here?"

"Yeah, I live somewhere else," Blondie said. "I don't live here but I'll go get the guy who does live here."

This must be some party. I wonder if everybody here is as drunk as this girl?

Blondie left the front door standing open while she went to get the homeowner. I took a couple of steps away from the front door onto the walkway. All I wanted to do was to make sure that everything was okay and tell the guy to keep the noise down. I could still see into the house down a long hallway. I saw a guy come walking down the hall towards the front door. Walking next to him was a dog the size of a small horse.

As I have mentioned before, many people who have dogs aren't smart enough to put them away when the police arrive. I knew what was about to happen and tried to create some distance between me and the Great Dane that was about to charge me. About the time, Scott, the drunk homeowner got to the front door, Lex, the big dog, had picked up my scent and ran out into the yard barking and looking for the stranger.

I had retreated down the walkway about twenty feet. Lex ran out in the front yard looking for me. He spotted me on the sidewalk and charged me, barking and growling. Scott yelled something at the dog, but Lex did not seem to understand drunk. This was a full sized Great Dane. He came up to my waist and probably weighed a hundred and fifty pounds.

When Lex was about ten feet away from me, I drew my Smith .45 pistol and fired a shot. Instead of dropping dead at my feet, however, the big dog started yelping like a puppy, skidded to a stop, and then turned and ran away. I had missed. *How did I miss a dog the size of a compact car from less than ten feet away?* Scott started yelling, "You shot my dog! You shot my dog!"

Thinking quickly, I said, "No, I didn't shoot him. I just fired in front of him to scare him away." I wasn't going to admit to this drunk that I was a terrible shot.

It took a moment for that to register. "You mean you didn't hit him?" Scott asked.

"Of course not," I said. "Do you see any blood?"

He stumbled over and looked around where Lex had been. My bullet had struck the ground in front of him. I told Scott that he needed to keep his dog on a leash. "If he charges me again, I won't miss," I warned him.

That pretty much ended the party. Scott and a few of his drunk friends went walking around, looking for Lex. Now I had to go and tell my Lieutenant that I had cranked off a round at a dog and missed. I met Lieutenant Bobby at the precinct and told him what had happened.

"You missed a Great Dane from how far away?" he asked.

I hung my head. "Less than ten feet."

"That is pretty embarrassing," he said.

Thanks boss. Stick the knife in and turn it.

I completed the report to document discharging my service weapon. I caught hell for the next couple of days in regards to my poor marksmanship. Everybody became a comedian. "Hey, Spell, if I get taken hostage, aim at me when you shoot. That way, maybe, you will hit the hostage taker."

"If Spell gets in a shooting, make sure you are behind him. There is no telling where his rounds are going!"

The only thing that I can figure is that with the Great Dane charging me, I just rushed the shot and jerked it. Even though Lex was a big dog, he presented a narrow target when viewed straight on. I would like to think that I would have nailed him if I had another chance. At any rate, I was at the firing range on my next off days working on my marksmanship.

If you have ever watched *America's Funniest Videos*, you know that the video usually involves an adorable kid or animal doing something cute or a guy getting hit between the legs with a ball or falling down. Well, I've had a couple of moments in my career that would have at least gotten me an honorable mention on that show.

During one of our other ice storms (See *Inclimate Weather and Idiots*), I was working a two car accident in which one car slid on the ice and hit another car. No one was hurt but the road was blocked while I wrote up the accident report and waited on tow trucks. There was a line of traffic waiting to get through but the road was closed until we could get the wrecked cars removed.

I finished the traffic citation for Too Fast for Conditions for the driver who caused the wreck. He was standing beside his smashed up car. I got out of my police car and started shuffling towards him. I thought I was being cautious on the ice but my feet went out from under me and I landed hard on my back. My clipboard went skittering down the icy road. I was not hurt too bad. My ballistic vest had cushioned the fall. I managed to get to my feet. The two drivers involved in the accident came over and helped me get up. One of them retrieved my clipboard and I issued the at-fault driver his citation.

"You mean I'm getting fined for having an accident on this ice?" he asked.

"That is exactly what it means," I answered and slowly, painfully, made my way back to my car. I am sure all the waiting motorists had a great story to tell at dinner that night.

Another memorable spill happened about six in the morning near Snellville. I was finishing up the midnight shift and was heading back to the precinct. I noticed that the car in front of me had expired registration. It had been expired for three months so I advised the dispatcher of my pullover and turned on my blue lights. We pulled into the parking lot of a convenience store, just up from the precinct.

Before I had even come to a complete stop, the driver's door of the violator's car came flying open and a white male bailed out and started to run behind the convenience store. I hurriedly advised the dispatcher that I was in a foot pursuit as I was opening the door of my police car.

It was not quite daylight yet so I grabbed my flashlight and stepped out of the car.

The violator was a young white male and he had a big head start on me. As I was running past the front of my cruiser, I lost my balance and fell flat on my face. I didn't trip over anything. I just stumbled and fell down. I felt pain in my knees and both hands. I blocked it out and pushed myself up and continued after my fleeing bad guy.

Behind the convenience store, there was a small field that connected to the road our precinct was located on. That was the direction the guy was running. I saw him run out into the field. The problem with this field, though, was that it was impassable by anything but rabbits and deer. It was covered in briars that were as high as five feet. As the guy tried to run through these thick briars, I could hear him squealing in pain and cussing. I was not about to follow him into that.

Since it was near shift change, there were several officers driving right by the field heading to the precinct. They had heard me advise that I was in a foot pursuit. I could see the blue lights on the other side of the field as four or five police cars stopped. I gave them a physical description of the guy. I was not going to run into the briars. I would let my friends try and apprehend him as I called a tow truck to come and impound the guy's car.

After a couple of minutes, I heard a voice shout, "Here he comes!" This was followed by the unmistakable sound of something metal hitting something solid, like maybe a head. An officer called me on the radio and said they had my guy and they would bring him over to me.

The adrenaline had started to wear off by now and my knees and hands were starting to sting. I looked down. I had ripped the left knee out of my uniform trousers. Both of my knees and both of my hands were scraped up from where I had fallen. Thankfully, they were only superficial scrapes and were not serious injuries.

The bad guy, however, was another story. The officer brought him to me and I got him out of his police car and stood him against mine in the now crowded convenience store parking lot. I took the first officer's handcuffs off and put mine on him and then secured him in my police car. This perp looked rough. He was shredded from head to toe by the briars and was a bloody mess. He was wearing a ripped t-shirt and shorts and I could see that he was cut to pieces and bleeding from numerous briar wounds. On top of that, he had a small lump on his head from where he had run into an officer's flashlight.

It was daylight by now and the parking lot of the convenience store was full of people on their way to work. I ran the violator on the computer and found out why he had run. It had nothing to do with his expired registration. His driver's license had been revoked for Driving Under the Influence and he had multiple outstanding warrants. When the tow truck arrived, I stepped into the convenience store to wash my scraped hands as best I could before driving the guy to jail.

When I came out of the restroom, the clerk, Erlene, said, "Wow! What did that fellow do? You guys must have kicked his ass! He was really messed up!"

Erlene was a bit of a saucy one and this was clearly the most excitement she had had since she was robbed at gunpoint a few months before. "No, we didn't do that to him. He ran through the briars behind the store," I told her.

"Sure he did, honey. Sure he did," she said and winked at me.

21

Drunk on a Riding Mower

The police radio came to life alerting us to the unusual call of a man "acting crazy" on a riding lawn mower. *This has the makings of a Redneck Joke written all over it*, I thought. It was July of 2010, and I was the Afternoon Shift watch commander at the East Precinct. I had three Sergeants and twenty five officers assigned to my shift. My boss, Major Tom, had taken off the week of July 4th and had left me in charge as the Acting Precinct Commander. On those occasions when I was left in charge, I had the freedom to modify my schedule as I saw fit. On this particular day, I was working Day Shift. I had spent about three hours in the office catching up on some of the Major's e-mails and signing some reports for him. It was time to get out of the office and ride around for a while.

The East Precinct is located in Dacula. This is the most rural area of Gwinnett County. Much of the area is comprised of rolling hills, farms, and winding country roads. There are residential areas and subdivisions scattered throughout but it is always a beautiful area to drive around in. It is a pretty quiet region as far as crime goes. We respond to a lot of domestic calls and get our share of motor vehicle accidents, but all in all, it is a nice area.

After I left the office, I was driving down one of the many picturesque country roads that surround Dacula. That was when I heard the Day Watch officer get dispatched to an Unknown Medical call. The white male was driving a riding lawn mower in and out of traffic and people's yards. He had driven the mower through a few people's flower beds. The caller said that he was "not acting right," and was "acting crazy." According to the complainant, the male was either drunk or on drugs.

When I heard the address, I realized I was on the right street and was only about two miles away.

I advised the dispatcher that I would be responding as well. When I got to the area where the male on the lawn mower was supposed to be, I saw him come out of someone's yard and into the street on a large riding mower. He saw me but just kept coming right out in front of me and into the middle of the road. Officer Jonathan was pulling up from the other direction so we had the guy blocked in. Or so we thought.

The white guy on the mower looked like he was in his forties. He was wearing blue jeans, a blue t-shirt, and a black ball cap. He had long stringy brown hair. He was driving a real nice Toro mower. I could see a piece of chicken wire protruding from under the mower. *He must have picked up the chicken wire when he drove through someone's flower bed,* I thought.

When Officer Jonathan pulled up and turned his blue lights on, the suspect stopped. He looked back at me, and then he looked at Jonathan. Jonathan got out of his patrol car and started to walk over to the mower. I was starting to get out of my patrol car. I could hear Jonathan yelling to Mr Toro to turn the mower off. Before Jonathan could get too close, however, Mr Toro extended the middle finger of his right hand towards Jonathan and told him to go and do something physically impossible. He then engaged the cutting blade and aimed the mower at the officer. Jonathan quickly jumped out of the way and drew his taser. Mr Toro then rammed into the side of Jonathan's police car, putting scratches and dents all the way down the side. He then took off down the road on the riding mower.

I jumped back into my police car and drove around Mr Toro and blocked the road off about fifty feet further up. I requested additional backup units, turned on my blue lights, and got out of the car. I didn't want any traffic to come flying down the road and hit Jonathan, me, or Mr Toro. By this time, Officer Jonathan had run around and gotten in front of the mower again and was ordering the guy to stop. I yelled at Jonathan to use his taser on the subject.

The taser is a great weapon. It fires two prongs that stick into the person being tased. Thin wires connect the prongs to the taser itself. The suspect gets a five second burst of electricity that usually ends their aggressive behavior. Occasionally, a suspect will need to be given another five second burst, but most people comply after the first blast.

Mr Toro was slumped down in the seat of the riding mower. Jonathan knew that if he shot the taser at him from the rear he likely would have had one of the prongs hit the seat itself, or stick him in the back of the guy's head. That is never recommended unless it is a deadly force situation.

Now Jonathan had positioned himself in front of the mower so that he had a clear shot at the front of the suspect. I yelled at him again, "Tase him!"

Jonathan waited until the last possible second, just before the mower was going to run over him, before firing the taser. The two prongs hit the suspect in the chest. Mr Toro went rigid as the electricity went through him, but he did not fall out of his seat. His foot did come off the gas pedal and the lawn mower stopped in the middle of the road. As soon as the five second burst was over, however, Mr Toro grabbed one of the prongs and ripped it out of his chest. This would prevent Jonathan from shocking him again effectively unless he reloaded another cartridge.

I pulled my ASP expandable baton out of the scabbard and flicked it open. The suspect stood up and it was obvious that he was about to run. Just as he was stepping off of the mower, I swung the ASP as hard as I could and hit him just above the right knee. His leg buckled backwards and he turned to his left as if he might want to go that way now. I landed two more hard blows with the ASP on the side of his right leg. I grabbed a handful of t-shirt near his right shoulder and jerked him off of the lawn mower and slammed him down on the asphalt.

Jonathan stepped in and started to handcuff the guy. Mr Toro wasn't through fighting, though. He started to push himself up and was almost to his feet. I was still holding the ASP. I landed three more hard blows to rear of his right leg and he collapsed to the pavement. This time we got him handcuffed.

Because the call had originally come out as an Unknown Medical call, the fire department and an ambulance had been dispatched as well. They had pulled up just as we were having to get physical with Mr Toro. We quickly discovered that his main issue was that he was intoxicated. It was only ten thirty in the morning but he told us that he had already consumed a six pack of beer.

After someone has been tased, we are required by policy to have them checked out by paramedics. Since the paramedics were already on-scene, that made it easy. One of the paramedics asked me, "How many times did you hit him with that stick?"

"Maybe five or six," I answered.

Mr Toro heard this exchange and said, "And it hurt like hell!"

The paramedics checked him over and found that he was fine to be transported to the jail. He did walk with a noticeable limp. Officer Jonathan charged our new friend with a long list of offenses, including Driving Under the Influence, Aggravated Assault on Police Officers, Resisting Arrest, and Damaging Government Property (Jonathan's patrol car). While we were getting everything sorted out, Mr Toro's brother came to the scene. He became argumentative telling us his brother had some serious medical conditions and did not need to go to jail. He used some choice language with a couple of the other officers on the scene. They chose to ignore it and not arrest him.

Later in the day, however, a few of our enterprising young officers found out that Rodney, Mr Toro's obnoxious brother, had an outstanding Probation Violation warrant for his arrest. They drove out to the house and scooped him up. He wasn't happy about going to jail but at least he and his brother could spend some quality time together.

22

Nino and the Stolen Car

In September of 2010, I was the second shift watch commander at our East Precinct. One evening about eight o'clock, I was driving through the little town of Dacula. Traffic was still fairly heavy as people were coming home from work. As I was sitting in traffic on Harbins Road, I noticed a silver Nissan X-Terra backing out of the driveway just across the street from me. This was a house that we had been out to on some domestic calls. I knew that a Bosnian family lived there.

I entered the license plate of the X-Terra into the computer in my police car. The computer system was running slow and I did not get a return right away. As traffic started to move, I lost sight of the vehicle. About a minute later, the registration information popped up on the computer screen. The words, "Stolen Vehicle," jumped out at me. I immediately whipped the police car into a three point turn, forcing oncoming traffic to brake for me, and went back to look for the stolen car.

It was possible that the X-Terra had pulled out behind me and was sitting in traffic also. I scanned the traffic as I went by but I was betting that they had seen me and were going in the opposite direction. Sure enough, as I rounded a curve on Harbins Road, I could see the stolen car about ten cars in front of me. With traffic being as heavy as it was, I was going to have to wait until either the perp turned off, or some of the other traffic did.

I did not want to alert dispatch yet because I wanted to make sure that I had run the correct tag. It is always embarrassing when you make a traffic stop based on the wrong tag. As I have gotten older, my eyes are not quite as good as they used to be. I was pretty sure I had gotten it right but wanted to confirm it before I called in the cavalry to back me up.

After about two miles, several of the vehicles between us had turned off. There were were only two cars separating me and the stolen car. I got a glimpse of the tag in a curve and saw that it was the same one that I had run. The two cars between us then turned off and I was now behind the stolen X-Terra. I keyed up the police radio and gave the dispatcher my location and told her that I was behind a stolen vehicle and requested backup units. My intention was to just keep following them until I got a few more police cars with me and then conduct a felony traffic stop.

The driver of the X-Terra then made a sudden left turn into a shopping center. There was a grocery store and several restaurants there. The parking lot was packed. I followed the vehicle into the shopping center and updated the dispatcher on my location. This could be good or bad. With the parking lot as full of cars as it was, the perp may have just trapped himself. That turned out to be wishful thinking on my part. In the parking lot, the stolen car turned left and accelerated towards the back of the shopping center where there was another exit. I activated my blue lights and prepared to stop the car. I did not want to do this by myself, but I knew that my closest backup unit was still several minutes away.

As it turned out, there was another police car in the parking lot. The Dacula City Marshal, Marshal Steve, was there helping a citizen that had locked their keys in their car. He was on the same radio frequency as us and had heard my radio traffic. Marshal Steve had retired from our agency a couple of years earlier as a Major. He had found retirement to be a bit boring and he was enjoying his job with the City of Dacula.

As I activated my blue lights, Marshal Steve pulled in front of the stolen vehicle blocking the lane. I stopped about ten feet behind it and had just gotten out of the police car. The X-Terra had stopped between the two police cars. I drew my pistol and yelled at the driver to turn off his vehicle. I saw the backup lights come on and the stolen car's tires squealed and smoked as it started quickly backing up towards me. I dove back into the police car, holstering my pistol. The X-Terra slammed into the front of my cruiser and actually came up on the hood. The X-Terra sits fairly high off the ground so the amount of actual damage to the police car was not as bad as it would have been if it had been a vehicle lower to the ground. The driver of the stolen car then jerked the steering wheel to the right and accelerated. At the same time, the passenger door came open and a teenage girl came diving out of the X-Terra. The stolen car then cut through the only opening available, between two parked cars, and then sped towards the other side of the parking lot and another exit. I found out later that Marshal Steve had grabbed the girl that had jumped out of the stolen car and taken her into custody. That turned out to be a very important decision.

I advised the dispatcher that the stolen car had rammed me and I was in a vehicle pursuit. Our pursuit policy does not allow us to chase someone just because they are in a stolen car. Because the subject had deliberately rammed my police car, however, I now had an Aggravated Assault on a Police Officer charge. I could now chase him until we caught him. As it turned out, it was a fairly short chase.

He turned right out of the shopping center and accelerated to about seventy miles an hour. He would have had a chance to outrun me if he had stayed on the main road. Instead, after about a mile, he made a sudden left turn into a residential neighborhood. There was no way out of this subdivision. I turned in behind him with my blue lights flashing and my siren blaring. Fortunately, there were no children out playing and the streets were deserted.

The next thing that happened was something right out of a movie. The X-Terra started slowing down. Instead of stopping, though, the driver jumped out of the still moving vehicle at about fifteen miles an hour. He hit the ground running and never missed a stride. I was still about fifty yards behind him. I got a good look at the guy but had no chance of chasing him down. He was a big white guy. He was wearing black shorts and a white, long sleeve t-shirt. For shoes, all he had on were flip flops. As I got up to where he had jumped, I saw him running through a backyard and vault a six foot privacy fence like it was not there.

The still moving stolen car kept going down the street eventually taking out two mailboxes and smashing into a cable box in front of someone's house. That is where it came to rest. I stopped behind it, turned its engine off and advised dispatch of my location and the suspect's description. By now a number of other officers were in the area responding to my first radio transmission about a stolen car. They established a good perimeter in an attempt to force the suspect to stop running. The police K9's were on their way and hopefully they would be able to track the suspect.

Sergeant Randy, my senior sergeant, came to the location and took charge of the search. He found out where every officer was and marked their locations on a map. The goal on a search like this is to surround the area with enough officers so that the suspect can't get through the perimeter. Within a few minutes, a good perimeter had been established. Two police dogs responded and we had Air One, the police helicopter hovering above us. *There is no way this guy is getting away*, I thought. Once again, I turned out to be wrong.

While Sergeant Randy was coordinating the search, I looked through the stolen car. I found a bag with about a half ounce of marijuana in the center console. Unfortunately, there was no ID for the suspect in the vehicle. I thought it was odd that the keys were in the X-Terra. Most stolen cars are hotwired. Usually, if the keys are in it, the victim was one of those mentally deficient people that leave their car running while they run into a convenience store for a pack of cigarettes or a cup of coffee. When they come back out, they are surprised to find that someone has "borrowed" their car. I requested a tow truck to come and impound the X-Terra.

Marshal Steve drove over to where we were at. He had the girl that had jumped out of the stolen car. She was handcuffed in his backseat. He told me that she was not being very talkative. I took her out and secured her in one of our police cars. She told me her name was Emira and she was seventeen years old. There are many different ways to interview people to get the information that you want. If you are too nice, the suspect thinks that you are a pushover and will give you false information because they think you are too stupid to know the difference. If you are too hard, the suspect generally clams up. You can threaten them all you want, but you probably will not get much out of them. It is generally best to strike a tone in the middle, firm but fair. It is also good to know how to use the suspect's fears to motivate them.

I sensed that Emira was scared. She was trying to put on a tough exterior but at seventeen she was unable to mask her fear. I wanted the name of the driver of the stolen car. I knew that she knew it but that she did not want to give it up. She just looked at the floor and said, "I don't know the guy's name."

I let her know what she was facing. If I did not get the name of the driver of the stolen car, I was going to charge her with being in possession of it. This got her attention. "But I wasn't driving," she said.

"It doesn't matter. You were in a stolen car. That is more than enough to charge you with the crime," I told her. "This is a felony that will follow you around the rest of your life. That is, after you get out of jail."

I dramatically slammed the back door of the police car and walked off to let Emira think about that for a little while. Sergeant Randy informed me that the police K9's were working a strong track on the suspect. Air One was equipped with a FLIR device that was able to locate suspects, even at night by picking up their body heat. As of yet, the helicopter had not located him.

I spoke to the residents that had had their mailboxes smashed by the stolen car. I got their names and information to include in the report. The wrecker arrived to impound the vehicle. The marijuana was secured in an evidence bag.

It was time to talk to Emira again. I told her, "I really don't want to charge you with this stolen car. The problem is, right now, you are the only one I have in custody so you are going to take the rap for it."

She looked at me and said, "His name is Nino. He is a friend of my brother's. He was at the house you saw us pulling out of. That is where I live. We were just going to get some food. I didn't know the car was stolen." *Now we are getting somewhere*, I thought.

"What is Nino's last name?" I asked her.

"I only know him as Nino," she said.

"Let me see if I can verify what you are telling me," I told her. "If I find out that you are lying to me, you are done. Do you understand? If you work with me, I'll try and help you. If you lie to me, I will charge you with everything I can find."

"I'm not lying," she said. "His name really is Nino. I know he has been in some trouble with the police before, but that is none of my business."

I closed the back door of the police car and went to work with the little bit of information that Emira had given me. Marshal Steve had taken her cell phone from her when he had taken her into custody. I took a look at her contact list. I quickly located a "Nino baby," in her contacts list. They had exchanged quite a few phone calls. I was going in the right direction but I needed a last name if I was going to charge Nino with all of the violations that I had on him.

At that moment, my own cell phone rang. "Is this Lieutenant Spell?" an unfamiliar voice asked.

When I told them that it was, the voice identified himself as a Deputy with our Sheriff's Department's Fugitive Squad. He said, "I hear you had a run in with our boy, Nino, tonight. We have been tracking him for two months and haven't been able to catch him yet."

The Deputy went on to give me Nino's full name and other pertinent information. The physical description that he gave me matched the guy that had run from me. He said that Nino was wanted for a host of felony charges, including another count of Aggravated Assault on a Police Officer, another count of Motor Vehicle Theft, Burglary, and felony Criminal Damage to Property. The Deputy told me that Nino was supposed to be a real dangerous guy who had told friends that he would not go back to jail. "Either the police will kill me, or I'll kill the police," he had been reported to say. *Sounds like a great guy*, I thought.

Sergeant Randy updated me on the search and said that it looked like Nino had slipped through the perimeter. The guys had done a great job but Nino had had a head start on us. He had gotten away. I was disappointed but at least I knew who he was. I could go and secure a number of warrants to go along with the ones that he had pending. They had searched for almost two hours and the police dogs were exhausted and the helicopter had not seen our suspect. I told Sergeant Randy that they could break down the perimeter.

While I still did not believe that Emira had told me everything she knew about Nino, she had provided me with some important information. I went back over to talk with her again. I told her that because she had helped us, I was not going to charge her with the stolen car. She was only going to be charged with Misdemeanor Possession of Marijuana. She would have had equal access to the marijuana that I found in the stolen car. She was still going to jail but was only looking at a fine and probation when she went to court. Emira was visibly relieved and actually thanked me for not charging her with the stolen car.

I had an officer transport Emira to the jail for me. I went to Headquarters and put the marijuana into the evidence room. The Motor Vehicle Theft Detective that had been working the case of the stolen car that I had jumped Nino and Emira in called me. We compared notes on what he had already done in his investigation and I told him about Nino and what I had learned from Emira and the Deputy with the Fugitive Squad. The Detective told me that he had suspected Nino's involvement but had not charged him yet.

The Detective told me that Nino had stolen the X-Terra and a Honda Accord from a fitness center that he was a member of. It was one of those franchise gyms with multiple locations. If you are a member, you can work out at any location. Nino's method was to go into the gym and work out. When he finished, he would grab a handful of keys off the key rack near the front door. He would then go out into the parking lot and push the buttons on the key bob listening for a car alarm to disengage. When he found the right car, he would drop the extra keys in the parking lot and leave in the stolen vehicle. The Accord and the X-Terra were stolen from two different locations of the same fitness center.

When the Accord was stolen, there were no witnesses. The Detective received access to the health club's data base and saw who had checked in during the times that the vehicle was taken. Nino was one of the only male members that had checked during those times. He was definitely the only member with an extensive criminal history. The Detective obtained a picture of Nino from the health club's files.

There was only one witness who saw Nino taking the keys on the day that he stole the X-Terra at the other health club. A member of the gym saw what was going on and thought it was strange, but not strange enough to call the police or even alert the management of the gym. When it became known that one of the other member's vehicles was stolen, the witness came forward and told management what he had seen. Management passed that information onto the police. The Detective put together a photo line-up that included Nino's picture. The witness picked him out as the one who he saw taking a handful of keys off of the key rack.

When I finished dealing with my evidence, it was time to go home. My plan was to secure warrants for Nino the following day. When I was driving into work the next day, my cell phone rang. "Lieutenant Spell? We got your boy Nino a little while ago," the Fugitive Squad Deputy told me.

The Deputy told me that they had tracked him to another one of his girlfriend's apartments. After they had confirmation that he was inside, they surrounded the apartment building. She lived on the second floor. The Fugitive Squad put two K9's outside on the ground below her second story patio along with several heavily armed deputies.

The rest of the team knocked on the door. When the girl opened the door, one of the deputies saw Nino on the patio behind her getting ready to jump. When he saw the two German Shepherds that were waiting below and hoping that he would jump, Nino paused. By that time, the Fugitive Squad was in the apartment and had shot him with two tasers. Nino collapsed to the floor and was quickly handcuffed before he could recover.

The Deputy filled me in on the other charges that Nino was going to have to answer for. I knew about the other stolen car. The other Aggravated Assault on a Police Officer had occurred about two months before. An officer at another one of our precincts had responded to a Suspicious Person call at an apartment complex. When the officer had arrived, she had encountered Nino sitting in the stolen Accord. She did not know that it was stolen. Nino was probably getting ready to do a drug deal or possibly even going to rob a drug dealer in the apartment complex. When the officer approached Nino and asked him to step out of his car, he aimed the stolen car at her and tried to run her over. Fortunately, the officer was able to jump out of the way. A witness at the scene identified Nino and provided information so that the officer was able to secure a warrant on him. The witness had also told the officer that Nino had an AK-47 rifle in the car.

The Burglary charge that was pending against Nino was from him breaking into his own parent's house. His parents had kicked him out earlier in the year because of the Felony Criminal Damage to Property charge. He and his father had had a disagreement and Nino had taken a golf club to his father's car. Nino had broken out all of the lights, windows, and mirrors, and pounded numerous dents into his father's vehicle. He had left before the police got there, but Officer Jonathan had taken the warrant out on Nino. Since then, he had broken into their house on several occasions when they weren't at home, stealing food, money, and other things that a criminal on the run needs.

After getting the download from the Deputy I obtained a number of warrants on Nino. He was charged with Possession of a Stolen Car, Aggravated Assault on a Police Officer, Damaging Government Property (my police car), Possession of Marijuana, Fleeing and Attempting to Elude a Police Officer, Reckless Driving, Suspended Driver's License, and Hit and Run for the mailboxes that his unattended vehicle knocked over.

I got the satisfaction of personally serving Nino with each of the warrants. He was in a holding cell and still wearing the same clothes he had fled from me in. I noticed right away that his legs were a mess. Both legs, from the knees down were a bloody mess from running through the woods at night in flip flops. I made him get up and walk over to the door of the holding cell. He limped over and I read off each of the new charges. I asked him if he had any questions. He just hung his head and started to go sit down.

"Hey, Nino," I said.

He looked back at me. "You have a nice day," were the words he heard as the door of his holding cell slammed shut.

23

Firepower

ONE THE THINGS THAT fascinates many people about Law Enforcement is the fact that we are the branch of government that carries guns. I realize that the military carries bigger guns, but they do not walk around the United States armed. Police officers do. Hollywood has done much to cultivate this interest through movies and television shows about police officers. The *Dirty Harry*, *Lethal Weapon*, and *Die Hard* series were great entertainment but really did not teach us anything about police work. The body counts are high in most Hollywood police movies and TV shows. In reality, most police officers will go through their entire career and never be involved in a shooting. Another irony is that many Hollywood producers, directors, and actors are anti-gun, yet consistently make movies that glorify gun violence.

The concerted attack against the Second Amendment has done much over the last thirty years to create a climate of fear in regards to firearms. Because people are ignorant about guns, they are scared of them. This fear is then passed on to their children and the cycle continues. One of my greatest joys over the years has been to teach firearms familiarization, safety, and marksmanship to citizens and to see many people overcome their fears.

I do like guns and have enjoyed hunting and recreational shooting for many years. My children were raised around guns and were taught the basic elements of firearms safety and marksmanship from a young age. Both of my daughters are excellent shots and I gave them pistols of their own. Guns are the great equalizer and I feel better knowing that my girls have the ability to defend themselves.

In this chapter, I am going to discuss some of the different weapons that I used during my Law Enforcement career. If you are not a gun person or you are not knowledgeable about some of the makes and models that I mention, feel free to Google them if you want to see what I am talking about. If it sounds like I am a little passionate about the guns I carried, I probably am. Every day that I strapped that gun around my waist, I knew that there was a possibility I would need it to defend my life or someone else's. It is easy to get attached to a "friend" like that!

My first issued firearm was a revolver. Most police departments still carried wheel guns when I started back in the mid-eighties. We were issued the stainless steel Smith & Wesson Model 681 Combat .357 Magnum. This was a beautiful six shot revolver. Like a guy's first girlfriend, this gun will always have a special place in my heart. The .357 magnum is a great caliber with tremendous stopping power. Not many people walked away after they were hit by one of those rounds.

While the gun itself shot great, the fact that it was a revolver presented a couple of challenges. First of all, it only held six rounds. Six bullets are not nearly enough in an extended firefight. When I entered the Law Enforcement arena, the average number of shots fired in an encounter was only about two to three. Over the years, that number has consistently gone up, along with the fact that officers are often contending with multiple assailants.

We were only issued a total of twelve bullets for our revolver. Six were loaded into the gun and the other six were to be kept loose in our pocket. This brings up the second challenge of carrying a revolver: reloading it. We were trained to reload one round at a time. If you really practiced, you could reload two rounds at a time. In a stressful situation, however, one of the first things that you lose are your fine motor skills, like putting a small round cartridge into a small round cylinder in the gun.

Many other police departments that carried revolvers issued their officers speed loaders. These are a handy-dandy little contraption that allows you to load all six bullets at once. A speed loader allows officers to perform a reload in around two seconds. Speed loaders can be worn on the duty belt for easy access. Most departments issued their officers two speed loaders. That provided the officer with an extra twelve rounds of ammunition.

My department, however, believed in giving the bad guys a sporting chance so we could not carry speed loaders. Six rounds in the gun and six loose in our pocket was what the Chief wanted. He did not think that speed loaders looked good on our duty belts so he outlawed them. Speed loaders were a bit bulky so it was not like you could carry them in your pocket. I am sure some of the guys did but if they had gotten caught, they would have been written up or suspended. I did carry a speed strip. This is a small piece of rubber that lets you attach all six of your extra rounds to it. It held the bullets and made reloading a little easier. It was not as good as a speed loader, but it was a lot better than fumbling around with loose bullets, spare change, and keys in your pocket.

After several years, we had a leadership change and our new Chief allowed us to carry speed loaders. We were all thrilled and felt like we had moved a little more into the Twentieth Century. By now, however, many departments were starting to transition to semiautomatic pistols.

When it came time for us to make the leap from revolvers to semi-autos, the Firearms Unit in the Training Division tested several different pistols. The primary benefit to having a semi-automatic pistol was that it gave the officer a lot more bullets. Some of the 9mm pistols gave the officer fifteen to eighteen rounds in his pistol with two additional high capacity magazines on his belt. Another advantage to the semi-auto is the fact that it allows the shooter to fire much faster. You still have to pull the trigger for every shot, but the trigger pull is much shorter than that of the revolver.

The Firearms Unit tested Sig Sauer, Glock, and Smith & Wesson pistols. Officers were encouraged to go to the range and test-fire the different pistols. After most of the officers in the department had fired all of the different pistols, they rated the Sig Sauers the most popular, with the Glocks being a close second. The Smith & Wesson semiautomatics brought up the rear, but only because someone had to be last. If we could have, many of us would have voted the Smith & Wessons out of the competition altogether. Of course, the Firearms Unit chose the Smith & Wesson pistols for our new duty gun.

I knew we would not get the Sig Sauer pistols. They are nice guns but they are very expensive. The price really matters when you are ordering several hundred of them. The Glocks would probably have been the best deal. Today, Glock has about seventy percent of the police market. Back then, they were still the new kids on the block and offered us an incredible deal. Our head firearms instructor, however, did not like the Glock. Even though most of the department ranked S&W last, that was what we got. Smith & Wesson has always made great revolvers. Their semi-automatic pistols, however, left a lot to be desired.

The Department did, at least, give the individual officers a choice of caliber. Caliber pertains to the size of the bullet that the gun shoots. Most everyone went with the 9mm version. There were a handful of us that elected to carry the S&W 4506. That is the .45 caliber flavor. A few officers chose the .40 caliber, but that was before the .40 S&W caliber was as popular as it is today. The 4506 that I carried had a magazine capacity of eight bullets. With the one loaded into the chamber, I had nine in the gun. I had two more eight round magazines in mag pouches on my belt. The 9mm pistol carried sixteen rounds of ammo but the .45 caliber bullets are twice the size of the 9mm. In this case, bigger is definitely better.

I carried the S&W 4506 for about ten years. It was an okay gun but I never became a fan of the S&W semi-autos. After carrying it for ten years, the firearms unit told me that it was time to retire it. Our department had been carrying semiautomatics for ten years now, and they were trying to get everyone using the same caliber. They issued me a S&W 5903 Tactical model in 9mm. This was a pretty good shooting gun, for a Smith & Wesson, and it had a rail on it so that a small tactical flashlight could be attached to the gun. I carried this pistol for about five years until we finally entered the Glock age.

I had been introduced to Glock pistols in the early nineties. I had attended a four day Glock Firearms Instructor's Course at their United States Headquarters in Smyrna, Georgia, and was captivated by the gun's simplicity, reliability, and accuracy. I began to carry a Glock as my off-duty gun. When my Department finally decided to carry Glock pistols, I was thrilled. The Glock Model 17 in 9mm is the pistol that is issued throughout the department. The magazine holds seventeen rounds of ammo for a total of eighteen in the gun. With two more seventeen round mags on our belts, we are pretty well armed.

You may have heard of the Glock when it first was introduced in America. The media quickly dubbed it, "The Plastic Gun," and said that it could pass undetected through airline security metal detectors. The frame of the gun is made of a heavy duty polymer, but it has consistently been shown to have enough metal present to register on a metal detector. This was another case of a biased news media trying to spread false information. As I mentioned earlier, Glock pistols have captured the majority of the Law Enforcement market. Glock pistols have a proven track record of being dependable, even under the most stressful and challenging conditions.

During my entire career with the police department, I have carried a backup gun. Most officers carry a second pistol hidden somewhere on their person. A backup gun is kind of like having a spare tire in the trunk of your car. I hope I never have to use it, but I am not going to leave it at home.

There are several reasons why officers carry backup guns. The first is that their primary weapon may malfunction. That is not likely, but I would not want to bet my life on a piece of machinery, even one as reliable as a Glock pistol. I can't imagine any worse feeling than to be in a life or death struggle and your gun says, "Click," instead of, "Bang."

Another reason that officers carry backup guns is that it can be difficult to draw your primary weapon when you are sitting in your police car. My backup gun is much easier to get to when I am sitting in the cruiser. Ideally, I don't want to confront a suspect while I am still sitting in my car. Stuff happens, however, and sometimes situations develop quickly or people walk up to us while we are sitting in a parking lot working on a report.

A third reason why officers carry backup guns is that it gives us another option if we were to run out of bullets. That would be a rare situation in which an officer expended all of his issued ammo. If it did happen, however, the officer could draw his backup and still be in the fight.

For the first half of my career, I carried a snub-nose revolver as my backup gun. Those are still the choice for many officers. They are small, easy to conceal, and the .38 Special caliber is usually a fight stopper. Small revolvers have also shown themselves to be very reliable. The biggest drawback to the small revolvers is that they only hold five rounds.

I finally gave up my backup revolver and started carrying the compact Glock Model 26. To me, this is the perfect backup gun. It holds eleven rounds of ammo and is just like the bigger Glock, except for its size. The full size Glock magazines also fit the smaller gun. If my Glock 17 duty gun were damaged, it is a great feeling knowing that I can stick the seventeen round mag in my Glock 26 backup gun and continue to fight. Another consideration was that the small Glock just outshot the small revolver. I took them both to the range and put them through their paces. The Glock shot much tighter groups, much faster.

Along with my service gun and backup gun, I also have always carried a shotgun in the police car with me. Early in my career, there were no rifles in Law Enforcement. The pump shotgun, however, has been involved in police work for many years. The shotgun provides devastating firepower up close and has ended more than one shootout. More than one bad guy has given up after hearing the distinctive sound of a shotgun being racked. There is no other sound quite like it and it can either be reassuring or terrifying, depending on which side of the gun you are on.

Early in my career, I assisted on a felony traffic stop of a van. The two men in the van were bank robbers and were considered to be armed and dangerous. We had them boxed in and surrounded. They weren't getting away. Both of them were hardened criminals who had spent many years each in prison. They knew that we had them so they just tried to make a joke of the situation. They laughed and yelled insults at us as we were getting them out of the van at gunpoint. I was behind a police car on the passenger side of the van. I had my shotgun out. The passenger yelled a few choice expletives at me as he was getting out. He then turned back, like he was going to reach for something in the van. The rack of my shotgun carried over all the other noise. The passenger bank robber understood that sound to mean, "I'm about to get shot by a shotgun!" He immediately became very compliant and his manners improved considerably.

Shotguns are great, and we are armed with good handguns. Many officers in our department, however, still felt that we were under armed. Bad guys were starting to pull out heavier firepower and we all felt that we needed to have access to rifles. The fear by many police administrators, however, was that rifles were too dangerous. I know, it sounds ridiculous. They give me a pistol. I can carry a shotgun. They give me a two thousand pound car to drive around in, but God forbid that the line officers be able to carry rifles. They might hurt someone.

In February of 1997, an incident took place in North Hollywood, California, that made police departments all over America take a closer look at how they were arming their officers. Two heavily armed men, both clad in body armor from head to toe, robbed the North Hollywood branch of the Bank of America. When confronted by the police as they exited the bank, a shootout ensued that lasted almost forty five minutes.

The police were armed with .38 Special revolvers, Beretta 9mm pistols, and at least one shotgun. The bad guys were armed with AK-47 rifles and AR-15 rifles. During the long shootout, around three thousand rounds were fired. Eleven police officers and seven civilians were wounded. Both of the perps were eventually killed, but that did not happen until the SWAT Team showed up and returned fire with their own AR-15 rifles. Both of the suspects had been hit multiple times, but their body armor had stopped all the pistol and shotgun rounds. The rifle rounds, however, had no trouble at all getting through the body armor.

After this incident, and a few others that were not as high-profile, many police departments began allowing their officers to carry rifles. My department first required us to take an intensive week long Rifle Course and then qualify with the gun on the last day. After that, we could carry the rifles in our police cars. Most departments use the AR-15 rifle in the .223 caliber because it is the civilian version of the military's M-16 rifle. It is easy to use and to maintain.

The rifle is not the weapon that you pull out of the car on every call. They only come out on the most serious of situations. As a department, we have had a few shootings in which the rifles came into play and took out bad guys. I have the honor, however, of firing the first rifle shot in the line of duty after we started carrying them. It was not against a person, though. It was against a cow.

I was working the night shift out of our Buford Precinct. Officer Craig was dispatched to a call of loose cows in the road. This was a rural area of the county and we got calls like this regularly. The problem with loose cows was that if you were driving down the road, singing along with the radio or talking on the phone and not paying a lot of attention, you could have a very bad night. I have worked a number of accidents over the years where motorists have collided with cows, horses, and especially deer. Deer do a lot of damage to the car, but it is rare that the occupants of the car are ever hurt. Cows and horses are another story. They are big enough to cause serious injury and even death to the unfortunate soul that runs into them.

The dispatcher told Craig that there were three black and white cows walking down the left shoulder of the road. As he neared the area where they had last been seen, he saw two cows standing on the opposite shoulder of the road. *The dispatcher said there were three cows*, he thought. *I wonder where the third one is?* At that moment, the missing bovine stepped off of the right shoulder into the path of Craig's police car. Fortunately, he was not going that fast, but it was still a shock to slam into the large animal. It destroyed the front end of the police car and deployed the airbag, but Craig was not hurt. He called the dispatcher and alerted her and his Sergeant to what had happened. The cow that he struck merely wandered over to where its mates were hanging out.

The Sergeant and Lieutenant both went to the scene to help out. They were able to locate the animals' owner. He came to the scene with a trailer and quickly loaded the first two cows into it. The third one, the one that had been hit, did not want to go anywhere. It was obvious that the animal was hurt but the injuries did not appear to be life-threatening. Every time the animal's owner went towards him, the cow would run down the road a short distance and then stop. At one point, the animal even lowered its head and indicated that it would butt anyone that got too close.

The police on the scene tried for around an hour to corral the angry animal. The owner realized that he was already liable for the damaged police car. It was just a matter of time before this animal caused another accident. The cow's owner finally told Lieutenant Paul, "You guys are going to need to shoot that thing before it hurts somebody or causes another wreck."

Lieutenant Paul knew that I was the only officer on the shift with a rifle so he called me to the scene. They briefed me on the situation and what needed to be done. The cow's owner told me that a head shot was the preferred method of shooting them. If I shot it in the body, it would probably run before dying and there was no way to predict which way it would run.

The owner told me to aim at the center of the skull, about six inches above the eyes. "That is where the brain is," he said.

As I was trying to set up to take the shot, the animal kept walking around. This forced me to readjust so I could aim for the spot the owner told me to shoot for. Finally, the cow stopped walking and turned to looked at me. It was a very short, thirty yard shot and I squeezed the trigger. The bullet struck the animal exactly where it was supposed to: the center of the skull, about six inches above the eyes. It was like someone flipped a light switch. The rogue cow dropped to its side, kicked twice, and was no more. We were all suitably impressed with the AR-15's performance.

As you can see, things have changed a lot over the last thirty years. Technology is constantly changing and improving the tools that a police officer uses to do their job. In the end, however, things really haven't changed that much. It still comes down to a brave man or woman who has sworn to protect and serve their community. It really does not matter what kind of gun the officer is holding in their hand. It just matters that they have the mindset to do their duty no matter what.

Epilogue

As I was writing and organizing this book, I had a nagging question in the back of my mind. I am a pretty straight-thinking, logical kind of guy. So, why did I not write *Street Cop* or *Street Cop II: Reloaded* more chronologically? In both books the stories ended up being grouped together in a way that flowed narratively, but jumped around chronologically.

One night, as I was sitting around the Roll Call table after shift with one of my senior Sergeants, it dawned on me. These books are written and organized like two old veteran cops telling war stories. One guy will tell a story that will stimulate memories in the other guy and then he will share one. This can go on for hours depending on the quality of the story teller and the interest of the audience.

If you ever have the honor of watching two military vets or a couple of crusty old cops sitting around swapping stories, consider yourself fortunate. Buy them another round of drinks and then listen. Don't tell them about the time you got stopped for speeding. They could care less. Chances are you are in the presence of a couple of heroes. They would never announce that but if you listen to their stories, you will get a pretty good idea of the kind of person that they are.

Another question that I am asked a lot is, "What keeps you grounded? With all of the negative aspects of your job, what do you do to keep it from poisoning you?"

I think that there are three things that have been tremendous influences in my life. First of all is my relationship with Jesus. Not Religion, not Christianity, but the person of Jesus. I met him several years before I became a police officer and He is the One who gives ultimate meaning and purpose to my life. If that sounds like a crutch, so be it. All I know is that one genuine encounter with God will transform your entire outlook on life.

The second powerful influence in my life is my family. I have a wonderful wife that has put up with me for almost thirty years. She understands some of the unique challenges of a job in Law Enforcement. These include working odd hours, sometimes for years at a time and the stress of low pay, especially early in my career. My daughters have provided inspiration and joy as I have watched them grow into beautiful, talented women. My parents and brother (a career paramedic and fireman) have also always been there for me, cheering me on.

The other major influence in my life is my church. I realize that even reading the word "church" makes some people throw up in their mouths. For many people, the idea of going to church is akin to the idea of getting a root canal. All I can say is that my experience is nothing like that. For me, The C3 Church is my family. They have been there for us when we have gone through some difficult times. They have cheered me on in my successes. They are my best friends and I cannot think of any other group of people that I would rather do life with. I have never been in a boring service at C3. I am not sure the words "boring," "traditional," or "legalistic" are even in our vocabulary.

Anyway, these are the three greatest influences in my life. Thanks for reading. Check out our website at www.thestreetcop.com. Please feel free to connect with me on Twitter @davidspell and on Facebook. My blog is www.davidspell.wordpress.com. I write on a variety of subjects and would welcome your feedback!